Hello!

While visiting family in Florida, I once took a dinner cruise like the one Brenna and the gang take in this book. I was thrilled to see manatees slowly swimming in the warm Gulf waters below us. I was also happy to see boaters obeying the speed limits so their propellers wouldn't injure the lovely manatees.

I talked to the captain and learned that not all boaters were as careful as the ones we saw that night. When I started to interview manatee veterinarians, I was horrified by the stories they told of the injuries manatees suffered from fast-moving boats, and the senseless deaths. I wanted to write a story that would explain this problem and bring more attention to the endangered species.

Creatures like manatees depend on you and me to keep them healthy and their habitats safe. This is something that Brenna Lake understands better than most. Her entire family rehabilitates injured wildlife and fights to make the world safer for all creatures.

I hope you can find a way to help, too!

Laurie Halse Anderson

MANATEE BLUES

LAURIE HALSE ANDERSON

SCHOLASTIC INC.
New York Toronto London Auckland Sydney
Mexico City New Delhi Hong Kong Buenos Aires

Acknowledgments

Thanks to Doug Warmolts, Columbus Zoo and Aquarium; David
M. Murphy, D.V.M., Lowry Park Zoo; Maya Dougherty, D.V.M., Miami
Seaquarium; Tom Pitchford, Florida Marine Research Institute; and
Nancy Sadusky, Save the Manatee.

ISBN-13: 978-0-545-15300-3
ISBN-10: 0-545-15300-X

12 11 10 9 8 7 6 5 4 3 2 1   9 10 11 12 13 14/0

Printed in the U.S.A.   40

This edition first printing, June 2009

To April, Ryan, and Tiffany Stevens,
with lots of love from Aunt Laurie.

Chapter One

. . . .

Ladies and gentlemen, may I have your attention, please. We will be boarding U.S. Air flight 1072 to Tampa, Florida, in just a few minutes. Please have your boarding passes ready. Thank you."

The woman behind the check-in desk turns off the microphone and smiles at me. "Only five more minutes," she says. "Then you're on your way."

I'm going to Florida!

This is amazing. Me, Brenna Lake, who never goes anywhere, I'm about to get on an airplane and fly south. But that's not all—I'm going to hang out with manatees!

I did a report about manatees last year for science class, and I fell in love with them. Manatees are marine mammals like dolphins, but they are endangered. Their habitat has been invaded by humans, and it is getting harder and harder for them to survive. They get hit by boats, eat trash that people dump in the water, and are harassed by people who don't understand how wonderful they are. It's a really sad situation.

I went nuts on the report. I drew a map of Florida that showed where manatees live, designed a poster of their life cycle, and made mom and baby manatees out of clay. My teacher gave me an A+. She said I should think about being a marine biologist when I grow up.

And now I'll be able to see the real thing—a live manatee, gentle, sweet, and trusting—at the Gold Coast Rescue Center. My legs start to jiggle. I can feel a cartwheel coming on. *Keep cool, Brenna. Remain calm. OK, deep breath. Check out what everyone else is doing.*

The whole gang from the Dr. Mac's Place is here at the Philadelphia airport with me: Sunita Patel, David Hutchinson, Maggie MacKenzie, and Maggie's cousin, Zoe Hopkins. The grown-ups— my parents and Dr. MacKenzie—are chatting by the window. A sleek silver plane waits outside.

The five of us volunteers are totally different, but we all love animals. Sunita, our cat expert, is smart, shy, and sweet. David, on the other hand, is loud and goofy. He really cares about horses and is an excellent rider. Maggie is great with all our patients, but dogs are her favorite. Zoe moved in with Maggie and Dr. MacKenzie—or "Dr. Mac," as we call her—a few months ago. She's still getting used to living around so many animals.

I grew up with animals. My parents are wild-life rehabilitators. People bring injured or sick animals to us, and we take care of them until they're better. That's how I got Edgar Allan Poe, my pet crow. We rehabbed him after he was shot, but since he could never fly again, Dad let me keep him as a pet. I'm going to miss him while I'm away.

Dr. Mac is the veterinarian who owns Dr. Mac's Place. She's also Maggie and Zoe's grand-mother. She asked me and the others to volunteer at the clinic a couple of months ago. It was the coolest thing that has ever happened to me.

When she first asked me to go along on the manatee trip, I knew my parents would say no.

We don't have that kind of extra money. When they heard that Dr. Mac insisted on paying for everything, they were like, "No way, we don't take charity."

Dr. Mac came over for dinner and spent all night convincing them. She's a genius. She's made a bundle from her newspaper column and from patents on some veterinary equipment, and she told my parents she likes to spend it teaching kids about animals.

She's donated a lot of money to the Gold Coast Rescue Center, too. That's part of why we're going. Dr. Mac is hosting a fund-raiser for the center. It's run by Gretchen Linden, a former student of Dr. Mac's. Along with manatee rescues and research, the center rehabs other injured wildlife. All that costs big bucks, so this fund-raiser is important.

I fiddle with the manatee charm on my good-luck bracelet. I wish we were already there.

"What time is it, Sunita?" I ask. "This is taking forever."

"Relax," she says, checking her watch. "You still have a few minutes." She sighs. "I wish I could come with you guys."

Sunita was invited, but she has to go to her

grandparents' sixtieth wedding anniversary. It's the kind of thing you can't miss.

Maggie takes a lollipop out of her backpack. "Keep an eye on David," she tells Sunita as she unwraps it. "We don't want him wrecking the place while we're gone."

"Hey!" David protests. "I wouldn't do that. Besides," he grins, "I'll be busy with Trickster."

David isn't coming with us either. He has been working with a special horse at Quinn's Stables. He had already promised to help Mr. Quinn out at a competition this weekend. David wouldn't miss that for the world.

Sunita smiles. "We'll take care of the clinic. You guys take care of the manatees. Take lots of pictures, Brenna. Manatees are adorable."

"You should see all the film I have." I pick up the camera hanging around my neck and look through the viewfinder at Sunita and David. "Squeeze in together. Move closer to David, Mag."

Maggie leans next to David, sticks the lollipop in her mouth, and crosses her eyes. David holds up two fingers behind Maggie's head. Sunita, sitting on the other side of David, smooths her hair down neatly.

"Wait for me!" Zoe calls. She drops her magazine and runs around behind the others. She rests her chin on David's head and gives the camera a brilliant Hollywood smile.

Click! I snap a quick picture of my friends. "Perfect!"

The woman at the check-in counter picks up her mike. "U.S. Air flight 1072 to Tampa is now boarding all rows."

People all around us collect their briefcases and carry-on luggage before joining the long line to get on the airplane. An electric tingle starts in my toes and shoots up to my head.

This is it!

As Maggie and Zoe get in line with Dr. Mac, I walk over to Mom and Dad, still standing by the window that looks out onto the parked plane.

Mom hugs me first. "Have fun," she says. She tucks an escaped strand of brown hair behind my ear. "Be polite, watch your temper, and think before you open your mouth."

I sort of have a reputation for blurting things out—especially when I lose my temper—but not on this trip. "I'll be a perfect angel," I promise.

"Have a great time, kiddo," Dad says. He gives me a bear hug, his beard scratching my cheek.

"And hang on to that camera."

"I'll sleep with it around my neck," I say. "Here. Let me get a picture of the two of you."

Through the viewfinder, my parents look small, out of place in the airport terminal. They belong back home in our little forest.

I press the shutter release. *Click!*

"You'd better get going," Mom says. She gives me one more quick kiss. "Be a good girl," she says.

Suddenly I realize this is the first time I'll be away from them for more than a day.

I hug her tightly. "I love you."

I hurry to the door and give the attendant my boarding pass, then wave to everyone one last time.

"Bye, guys!" I shout, jiggling the bracelet on my wrist.

Mom and Dad wave back. David puts his thumbs up against the sides of his head and wiggles his fingers at us like antlers. Sunita mimics holding a camera and mouths, "Take pictures."

"Ready?" asks Dr. Mac.

"Let's rock!"

Chapter Two

. . . .

My first minute in Florida!

As I step out of the airport terminal in Tampa, the heat wraps itself around me. It's got to be one hundred degrees. The air is heavy and smells like the ocean, the sun so bright I have to squint.

Zoe fans her face with her magazine. "I forgot how hot it gets here in the summer. The best time to come to Florida is April, not July."

"This way, girls," Dr. Mac calls. "We've still got about a half-hour drive to Bay City ahead of us."

Maggie, Zoe, and I follow her to the rental-car parking lot, dragging our suitcases and backpacks. Dr. Mac is the mother duck, and we're the ducklings.

The attendant at the car lot, a young guy with a great tan and bleached-blond hair, gives Dr. Mac a form to fill out. While she's taking care of the paperwork, I look around. It's only a parking lot, but it's beautiful. Spiky plants with brilliant red and bright pink flowers grow along a low wall. Hidden insects whir and click, and seagulls cry overhead. The people walking by us are speaking Spanish, and a car radio somewhere plays salsa music. It couldn't be more different from home.

I love it.

Zoe flaps her magazine in my direction. "You look hot," she says. "What are you staring at?"

"I can't believe I'm really seeing palm trees," I say. "They look so weird. Don't they remind you of David's hair, the way the palm leaves stick out on the top?"

"Take a picture," Maggie suggests.

"Good idea." I take aim and shoot. *Click!*

"What are those birds, Brenna?" Zoe asks as she points overhead.

"Oh, my gosh. Snowy egrets!" I adjust the camera lens to bring the elegant birds into focus.

They have enormous white wings, S-shaped necks, and plumes on their heads—just like I've seen in Mom's bird books. They look like soaring ballerinas.

Before I can get the shot, the egrets disappear behind a billboard. *Darn.* I'll have to shoot faster.

The rental-car guy hands the car keys to Dr. Mac. "First time in Florida?" he asks with a friendly smile.

"First time anywhere," I answer.

"Are you going to Disney World?" he asks.

I shake my head. "Way better than that. We're going to Gold Coast Rescue Center."

"Never heard of it," he says.

Dr. Mac opens the trunk of the white sedan. "The girls are going to work with recuperating manatees."

The attendant lifts the suitcases into the trunk. "You came all the way down here to do that?"

"We're going to squeeze in a baseball game, too," Dr. Mac says. "I got us tickets for the Bay City Stingers and the Hurricanes."

"Yes!" Maggie pumps her fist in the air, almost smacking her cousin. "The Stingers have one of the best hitters in the league, Ronnie Masters. He used to play for the Philadelphia Phillies."

"We can watch baseball at home," I say, putting my suitcase next to Maggie's. "I want to spend all my time with the manatees."

The attendant closes the trunk. "It's probably a good idea," he says. "My girlfriend told me that manatees are dying off. There aren't that many left, you know."

• • • • • • •

The two-story stucco rescue center is bigger than I thought it would be, with a middle section and two wings that go off to the left and the right. A slow-moving river flows behind the center, shaded by tall oaks draped with spooky Spanish moss. Exotic birds screech from the top of the trees. The insects here are louder than at the airport, and it's hot and sticky, even in the shade.

"Welcome to the Gold Coast Rescue Center," reads a faded sign on the front door. "Bay City, Florida."

Dr. Mac told us that Gold Coast is a manatee critical-care center. It's certified to rescue injured or sick manatees and to rehabilitate and take care of them until they are healthy enough to be released into the wild. It's supposed to be a tourist spot, too, but we're the only visitors I can see. The cars in the parking lot are all in the "Reserved for Staff" spaces.

Dr. Mac tugs on the front door. It's locked. Maggie leans against the glass to peer inside.

"That's strange," Dr. Mac says. She knocks on the door. "Gretchen knew we were coming. I hope everything is all right."

"Maybe they're on a lunch break," Zoe suggests.

"Wait, here comes someone," Maggie says.

"Gretchen!" Dr. Mac exclaims.

A tall, muscular woman wearing a light blue sleeveless shirt and black shorts unlocks and pushes open the front door. Her blond hair is up in a bun. She looks like she's around thirty years old, but there are dark circles under her eyes. I bet she works really hard.

"J.J.!" the woman exclaims. "I thought I heard a car pull in. Sorry about the door." She gives Dr. Mac a big hug. "It's been nuts around here. I'll tell you about it later. These must be the girls."

Dr. Mac beams. "Maggie and Zoe, my granddaughters, and our friend Brenna Lake. Girls, this is Gretchen Linden, director of the center."

"I'm so glad you could come," Gretchen tells us. "Dr. Mac e-mailed me all about you guys."

"Gran has told us a lot about you, too," Maggie says.

"Thanks for inviting us," Zoe says politely.

Enough chitchat. "Can we see the manatees?" I blurt out.

"Patience, Brenna," Dr. Mac says.

"No, that's great," Gretchen says. "We like enthusiasm. This center was created to get people excited about manatees and other Florida wildlife. We need more people like Brenna."

I like this lady. She thinks the same way I do.

A thin man wearing khaki shorts and a gray polo shirt leans out the door. "Uh, Gretchen?" he asks.

"Carlos, come out and meet everyone," Gretchen says. "Carlos is the assistant director here. He's the best marine biologist in the state."

"We have an emergency," Carlos says, holding up a portable phone. "An injured manatee floating by Walker's Point."

Gretchen's smile vanishes. "A boat strike?"

"Sounds like it. The caller says it's cut and swimming on one side."

An injured manatee? My heart starts thumping.

Gretchen is all business. "Get the boats ready," she tells Carlos. "I'll be there in a minute."

I want to go with them.

Carlos jogs back inside, talking into the phone. Gretchen puts her hands on her hips and sighs. "Sorry, guys. Duty calls. I have to go."

Dr. Mac nods her head. "I understand. We'll head for the hotel. You can call us when you're free."

We're leaving? No way!

"Can't we go?" I ask.

Gretchen hesitates. "Brenna, this manatee was probably cut by boat propellers. It won't be nice to look at. But don't run off. I'll have one of the volunteers show you around."

The last thing I want right now is a tour. I follow Gretchen to the front door. "Gross things and injured animals don't bother me. We see them all the time at Dr.Mac's Place. Let me go with you." *Be polite, Mom said.* "Please?"

"Brenna," Dr. Mac says sternly. She's using that grown-up code voice, telling me to shut up and leave Gretchen alone. But I can't. Not when I'm this close to a real rescue.

"We came down here to learn about manatees," I say. "Isn't this the perfect thing for us to do?"

"We usually take two boats," Gretchen says slowly. "There's enough room, if you think it's all right, J.J."

Dr. Mac's right eyebrow creeps up a tiny bit as she studies me.

"I'll do whatever I'm told," I say. "Cross my heart and hope to die."

Chapter Three

● ● ● ● ● ● ● ● ● ● ● ●

The rescue center boats creep down the river at ten miles an hour. I thought we'd be rushing to the scene like a fire truck or ambulance, but we drive slowly so we can steer clear of any manatees. Fast boats and manatees just don't mix.

Gretchen drives the four of us in the lead motorboat, loaded with nets and medical equipment. The seats aren't exactly comfortable, and the heat is awful. We came dressed for an air-conditioned airplane ride, not a sauna bath. I'm sweaty and smelly, and I already have fifty million mosquito bites.

Don't think about the heat, I tell myself. *Get ready.* I check my camera: film loaded, lens cap off. I'm set.

Behind us, Carlos drives the *Gordito,* the center's special rescue boat, with four staff members on board to help. The *Gordito* is designed especially for work around manatees. The engine sits under the middle of the boat instead of hanging off the back end, and the propeller blades are shielded with a special guard to prevent manatee injuries. The back is cut low, almost down to the surface of the water, so a manatee can be hauled on board.

Gretchen fills us in on manatee behavior as we scan the water for our patient. "Manatees spend their days searching for food in rivers and canals and along the coast," she explains as she pilots the boat. "They're herbivores, which means they eat only plants. The average manatee eats one hundred pounds of vegetation a day. They're like vacuum cleaners."

"Wow!" Zoe says. "A hundred pounds!"

"I know," Gretchen says. "A lot of veggies, isn't it?" She pauses to steer the boat around a drifting log. "Manatees spend eight hours a day swimming and eating. They move very slowly and are extremely hard to see if the water is murky. If boaters are driving too fast, or not watching out for them—*boom!* Boat hits manatee."

"Wait!" I call out. "Is that it over there?"

A gray lump of something drifts in the current. Gretchen and Dr. Mac crane their necks for a better look, then Dr. Mac picks up a long pole from the bottom of the boat. She stretches out and prods the gray blob.

"False alarm," she says as she lifts the dripping thing in the air. "It's just a trash bag." She dumps the bag in the boat and puts the pole away. "Keep your eyes open."

"Do a lot of manatees get hit by boats?" Zoe asks.

Gretchen slows down a bit as we enter a sharp curve in the river.

"It averages out to about one boat strike a week," she explains. "Some manatees die from eating trash thrown into the water, like that bag. And they die of natural causes, of course. They're tropical animals and very sensitive to cold. If we have an unusually cold winter, the number of manatee fatalities goes up."

"Don't forget red tide," Dr. Mac adds. "That's a

kind of algae that killed a couple hundred manatees a few years ago."

"That's so depressing," I say.

She glances back at me. "I know. Florida manatees are our most endangered coastal mammal.
There are fewer than three thousand of them left
right now. That's not many."

"How much farther?" Maggie asks as she slaps
a mosquito on her arm.

"A little while yet," Gretchen says. "Walker's
Point is about a half mile from here." She keeps
her eyes focused on the water as she drives the
boat.

I scan the area with my camera. The river-
banks close to the rescue center were wild with
trees, shrubs, and vines, all draped with strands
of Spanish moss. But here the river is lined
with neatly mowed backyards. There are houses
everywhere, lots of them with private docks jut-
ting into the water. I didn't realize that manatees
lived so close to people.

I turn the camera from the houses back to the
water. The sun glints off the surface of the river,
making colors swirl and shift, murky blue to
pale green to stone gray.

Hang on. What's that?

"Gretchen, look over there!" I say, focusing the lens. The patch of gray in the water is striped with red. Blood.

"It's the manatee!"

"It's Violet!" Carlos shouts as he cuts the engine. "She's alive!"

Gretchen brings our boat alongside the injured manatee, drops the anchor over the side, and turns off the engine. Carlos does the same, positioning the *Gordito* so the back end faces the manatee.

Maggie, Zoe, and I crowd the side of the boat for a better look. The manatee is huge. She's longer than my dad is tall, and shaped like a seal: roly-poly round in the middle, then slimming down to a paddle for a tail. She's rolled up on her side. That can't be good. Manatees normally float straight up and down.

I can't keep my eyes from the horrible gashes that have opened up the skin on the manatee's back—seven deep, straight lines, four of them curving around her side. I shudder, then snap a picture. *Click!*

"Yep, definitely Violet," Gretchen says. She kicks off her sneakers and slips into a pair of rubber shoes.

"The manatee has a name?" I ask.

"We've treated her before. She's had a few run-ins with boats. Look at her tail," Gretchen says, pointing to its jagged edge. It looks like something took a bite out of it. "We identify manatees by their scars. That is definitely Violet."

Gretchen puts her hands on the edge of the boat and hops into the waist-deep water. Carlos and a couple of his staff do the same thing.

"What are they going to do?" Zoe asks Dr. Mac nervously.

"They need to examine Violet's injuries," Dr. Mac says. "If she's not hurt too badly, they can treat her cuts and release her to heal on her own."

Gretchen and Carlos talk quietly as they inspect the cuts on Violet's back. Carlos puts on a stethoscope and places it on the broad back of the manatee to listen to her breathe.

"She's so calm," Maggie says.

Dr. Mac frowns. "That's not good. It could be a sign that she's really run down and exhausted. Normally, she'd swim away from people."

Gretchen grabs a face mask and snorkel off the *Gordito,* puts them on, and ducks her head underwater. When she comes back to the surface and takes off the mask, her face is grim. She wades back to our boat, climbs in, and opens one of the medical kits.

"How is she?" I ask.

"She's in serious trouble," Gretchen says. "It's definitely a boat strike—the propeller marks prove that. She has a pneumothorax. The propeller probably broke a couple of ribs, and the ribs made a hole in the left lung. Air from the punctured lung is trapped in her chest cavity. That's keeping her rolled up on her side. She's like a cork floating on top of the water. We have to get her back to the center, or she'll die."

I have a million questions, but Gretchen is too busy to answer them.

Some of Carlos's staff are unfurling a big net. One of the men slowly drives the *Gordito* in a big circle, pulling the net so that it wraps around Violet. Carlos and Gretchen wade out of the way so they don't get caught in the net themselves.

"Dr. Mac, how are they going to get her out of the water?" I ask. "She must weigh a ton!"

"Probably close to a half ton," she replies. "They certainly can't pick her up the way we pick up an injured cat or dog. They'll use the net to pull her up into the boat. That's why the boat has no real back end—to make it easier to transport manatees."

I adjust the focus on my camera and snap a few shots of Violet being loaded onto the boat. It takes all six adults to pull her in by hand. Once she's secured, Gretchen wades over to us again.

"Brenna, do you want to ride along in the *Gordito*?" she asks.

"Are you kidding? Sure!" I bolt from my seat and raise my foot to climb into the water.

"No, hang on," Gretchen laughs. "Wait a sec. Carlos will bring the *Gordito* alongside."

When the rescue boat is right next to ours, I step into it. There's a tiny bit of room for me behind Carlos, right next to Violet's head. I sit down, and the boat heads slowly back to the center.

I can't believe I'm actually this close to a real live manatee!

Violet's leathery skin is gray like an old nickel and has bristly hairs on it. Algae and barnacles are growing on her back. When I did my report, I found out that fish snack on the algae that grows on manatees, like they're floating dinner tables or something.

I sneak a look at the deep propeller cuts on

her back and sides. I can see the white layer of blubber under Violet's skin. Those cuts must feel like the worst thing in the world. Manatees are sensitive to touch. They like to cuddle with each other and nuzzle with their funny snouts.

She opens her nose flaps and exhales, then inhales quickly. Manatees have to come to the surface of the water to breathe. That's part of the problem. When they're near the surface, they're more likely to get hit by boats.

"Here, listen to her lung for me," Carlos says, handing me his stethoscope and watch. He points to where I should listen, on the right side of her back. "You won't get any respiratory sounds on the left because that lung is punctured. She should be breathing about once a minute right now, her heart beating once a second. Let me know if it changes."

"I thought manatees breathed slowly, like once every fifteen minutes," I say as I fumble with the stethoscope.

"That's when they're sleeping. When they're swimming in the water, they breathe once every three minutes. Her heartbeat and respiratory rate are faster than normal right now because of the stress she's feeling," Carlos says.

I listen carefully. *Lub-dub...lub-dub...lub-dub.* Her heart beats like waves rolling up onto the beach. Her lung whooshes with a giant exhale, then quickly fills with air again.

Violet's eyes roll back to look at me. They're small, not much bigger than a pair of dimes, dark, wet, and soft like a deer's.

What is she thinking? Does she know we're trying to help her? Does she recognize Carlos from the last time he treated her?

"Can't we drive faster?" I ask.

Carlos shakes his head. "These are manatee waters," he says. "It doesn't do us any good if we hit another manatee while we're rescuing this one."

"But can't you do something? I mean, isn't she in pain?" When an injured animal comes into the clinic, Dr. Mac and Dr. Gabe treat it right away.

"Transporting her like this puts a lot of stress on her," Carlos explains to me. "If we started to poke and prod her now, that would make things worse. We have to get her back to the center before we start any treatment."

"Is she going to make it?" I ask.

Carlos glances down at the water before answering. "We're going to try our best, Brenna."

Violet closes her eyes and sighs. *Lub-dub...lub-dub...lub-dub.*

Hang in there, Violet. Don't die!

Chapter Four

• • • • • • • • • • •

When we finally get back to the rescue center, we dock the boats. Gretchen hops into a forklift with a small crane built onto the front end, and drives it to the edge of the dock. We sure don't have any equipment like that at Dr. Mac's Place!

Carlos and his staff slide Violet into the water, then onto a sling. They hook the sling up to the crane. Gretchen maneuvers the crane and carefully hoists Violet into the air. With Carlos walking next to Violet, the crane and its load slowly make their way through the open doors of the rescue center's manatee wing. The rest of us are close behind.

The manatee wing has two tanks, a large one with a glass wall that you can see through from the center's exhibition area, and a smaller behind-the-scenes tank that is connected to the larger one by a chute. Gretchen rolls the crane to the edge of the chute and waits while Carlos and the others climb down into it. At his signal, she lowers the sling until Violet rests on the floor of the dry chute. Gretchen grabs a red plastic equipment box and climbs down to join her patient. An assistant is already listening to Violet's heart and lung with a stethoscope.

"I suppose you want to watch the examination," Dr. Mac says knowingly.

I look at my friends. We're all thinking the same thing.

"You'd better believe it," I say.

We sit cross-legged on the cement floor above the chute and watch what's going on below us. Gretchen takes a clipboard out of the equipment box and hands it to one of the assistants, who starts writing.

"She weighs nine hundred pounds," Gretchen says.

"How does she know that?" I ask Dr. Mac.

"The crane has a scale built into it," she replies.

Gretchen and Carlos stretch a measuring tape from the tip of Violet's snout to the end of her ragged tail. "Two hundred seventy-two centimeters long," Carlos reads. They measure around Violet's tail, too. "Peduncle girth, one hundred seven centimeters."

"What's a peduncle?" I ask Gretchen.

She points to where Violet's body meets her tail. "The peduncle is the narrower area between the body and the tail paddle. It's the closest thing the manatee has to a rump. That's where we usually give injections." She moves up to Violet's head and points. "Can you see this indentation behind her head?" she asks.

"Yes," I say.

"It shouldn't be here. A healthy manatee has a fat, round head with no signs of having a neck at all. This"— she kneels down and points to the curve in Violet's head—"is what we call 'peanut head' because it's shaped like a peanut. It is a sign that she's dehydrated—she doesn't have enough fluids and nutrients in her body. I'm sure you know how dangerous that is."

Gretchen stands up. "Violet was probably hit by that boat a couple of weeks ago."

"Weeks ago?" I echo. "She's been hurt like this for weeks? That's horrible!"

"I agree," Gretchen continues. "She hasn't been eating and has gotten weaker and weaker from her injuries. She's lost a lot of weight and is worn out. Another day or so and she could have died."

"Are you going to give her an I.V.?" Maggie asks Gretchen.

When a patient at the animal clinic is dehydrated, Dr. Mac sets up an I.V. to send nutritious fluids right into the animal's bloodstream.

"Good question," Gretchen says. "But we can't do that with manatees. Their cardiovascular system is wired very differently from that of other animals. It helps them thermoregulate—control the temperature of their bodies—but makes it impossible to rehydrate them with an I.V. If she were a little stronger, we'd just let her eat and drink on her own. But because she really needs nutrients and fluids, we're going to put a tube down into her stomach and feed her that way." She turns to Carlos. "All set?"

Carlos holds Violet's head while Gretchen takes

a thin plastic tube and inserts it through Violet's right nose flap. The tube keeps going and going. It must be a long way down to the stomach.

"There we go," Gretchen says when she finally stops inserting the tube. "Do you have the funnel?" she asks Carlos.

"Right here," he says.

Carlos inserts a funnel in the end of the tube. Gretchen opens a plastic bottle of clear liquid and slowly pours it into the funnel. The liquid goes down the tube, into Violet's stomach. The manatee just lies there. She really must be sick. If anybody did that to me, I'd be out of there in a flash.

"Since she's so severely dehydrated, we're giving her the replacement fluid farmers use for sick cows," Gretchen says. "Hopefully, it will help her get her energy back." She pauses while the last of the fluid flows down the tube. "By tomorrow, we should be able to start feeding her a lettuce slush. The goal is to get her back to eating on her own as soon as possible."

"Lettuce slush? Yuck!" says Zoe.

While Carlos removes the feeding tube, Gretchen puts on a stethoscope and slides the end of it all the way down Violet's back.

"Why is she doing that?" Zoe asks Dr. Mac. "The lungs are up in the chest, not down there, right?"

"Manatees have unusual lungs," Dr. Mac explains. "They are very long and flat, extending all the way down the back. Large lungs help a manatee control its buoyancy, how high or low it floats in the water. Their bones help them, too. They are solid, not hollow like our bones. That makes them very heavy. By exhaling, the manatee can sink or dive deeper. By keeping her lungs inflated, she can float at the surface. These are great adaptations to the environment the manatees live in."

Gretchen takes the stethoscope out of her ears. "When we have an animal with an old pneumothorax like this, we have to worry about a dead lung," she says. "That's when the punctured lung has actually died and started to decay. It's bad."

"Does she have it?" I ask.

"I'm not sure yet, but I don't think so. Her breath smells pretty good, for a manatee. If she had a dead lung, we'd notice a rotting smell. When I X-ray, I'll see if there is any fluid in the chest cavity."

She turns to her assistant. "Left lung deflated,

left side pneumothorax, right lung strong, respiratory rate once a minute," Gretchen says. "Heart rate once a second." The assistant writes down all the information, just like we take notes for Dr. Mac and Dr. Gabe at the clinic.

Carlos fills a clean syringe with clear fluid from a glass vial. The needle on the syringe is enormous, at least three inches long. Then he sticks the needle just above Violet's peduncle and injects the fluid into her.

"That's an antibiotic," Dr. Mac says. "That will help fight any infection that Violet has. He's rubbing the area where he inserted the needle to distribute the antibiotics better."

"Wait a minute," Zoe says to Dr. Mac. "How come they haven't taken her temperature, or looked in her mouth, or checked her ears—all those things you do at the clinic?"

"They don't want to stress her body out any more than is absolutely necessary," Dr. Mac explains. "Dogs and cats are used to being touched by people and can tolerate more poking and prodding. There is a real art to treating wild animals. The vet has to watch the animal's behavior to figure out how she's feeling."

I can understand that. At home when we're

rehabbing a fox or deer, we have to do the same thing.

"Do you want to X-ray her now?" Carlos asks Gretchen.

Gretchen cracks her knuckles, surveying her patient. "I don't know. Her ribs are broken and her lung is punctured. Plus she has contaminated wounds and is fighting infection. She is one stressed puppy."

She looks up to where we sit, on the concrete above her. "To X-ray, we have to anesthetize her. She's very weak right now, and I'm afraid the stress of the anesthesia and additional movement will be too much for her."

"Let's tap the chest, flush her cuts, and patch them up," she tells Carlos. "She needs to chill out for a while. We'll tube-feed her every four hours and reassess her condition in the morning. If she's stronger then, we'll X-ray and do a serious cleaning of the prop wounds."

When the propeller cuts have been washed out, Gretchen and Carlos lay an enormous disinfectant-soaked bandage across Violet's side. It's bigger than a beach towel. Gretchen takes a tube of something out of her medical kit and dabs it on the edges of the bandage.

"Guess what this is," she calls up to us. "Superglue. It's the only thing that keeps these bandages on." She injects a local painkiller into the skin on Violet's back, then inserts a large syringe with a thick needle into her chest. She pulls up on the plunger of the syringe.

"That's tapping the chest," Dr. Mac explains. "She's removing the air that leaked into the chest cavity so Violet will be able to expand her collapsed lung again. I've done the same thing on dogs plenty of times."

When the chest tap is complete, Gretchen starts to clean up. "All right, gang, let's get this girl in the water."

The staff quickly pick up all the equipment from the floor of the chute and climb up the ladder. One of the assistants walks over to a small control box on the wall and pushes a few buttons. Water begins to flow into the chute.

When the water is as high as Gretchen's knees, it stops. She and Carlos remove the sling, which Violet is now floating over. They run their hands over the bandage to make sure it is holding.

"Looks good," Gretchen says. "Time for some peace and quiet, Violet."

She and Carlos climb out of the chute, bringing the sling with them. The assistant lets more water into the chute. When the chute is totally full, the door that leads to the exhibit tank opens, and Violet swims through it. She moves very slowly, more like she's swimming through Jell-O than water.

"Is she going to make it?" I ask.

Gretchen studies her patient. "We'll know better in a few days. Carlos will keep an eye on her for now. Why don't I show you around?"

Chapter Five

· · · · · · · · · · · ·

Gretchen leads us down the stairs to the middle of the rescue center, the exhibit area. The long glass wall of the manatee tank is the star attraction.

"Look at Violet!" I shout.

Under the water, she looks almost graceful. Her tail flaps once and she glides in front of us, her snout quivering and her right flipper swaying. She's not moving her left flipper, and the bandage covering her cuts looks weird in the water, but what counts is that it's still on and in the right place.

"Couldn't you just stay here all day and watch her?" I ask.

Gretchen grins. "Sometimes I do. I never get tired of looking at manatees."

There is a long bench in front of the glass wall for people to sit on, and lots of extra room to handle a crowd—but we're still the only visitors. There is a clear plastic donation box by the door. It has an inch of pennies, dimes, and nickels in it, along with some gum wrappers.

"I thought this was supposed to be a big tourist place," I say.

Gretchen looks over at the donation box. "We don't get many visitors," she says with a sigh. "The center needs more money for advertising. The center needs more money, period. Come on. I want to show you some other friends."

She leads us down the hall. "Although manatees are a big part of the work here, we take in all kinds of creatures." She opens a door. "Here's the hospital ward."

It looks like the recovery room back at Dr. Mac's Place, but bigger, and with a curious collection of critters. Various-size cages line two walls, a couple of refrigerators and some medical equipment run along the third, and sinks, cupboards, and a long counter fill the wall right next to the door. An examining table is in the middle of the room. Music plays from a speaker mounted near the refrigerator—country-and-western. Not my favorite, but maybe the animals like it. We're in the South, after all.

"Wow!" Maggie gasps. "Look at these guys."

These are not your average animal clinic patients. There are lizards, snakes, turtles, giant birds, and a couple of opossums.

"Aren't they great?" Gretchen says. She walks over to a large glass cage where a long red snake has coiled itself over and around rocks and branches. We all kneel down to get a good look. The snake flicks his tongue out at us.

"This is Ralph," Gretchen says. "He's a red rat snake."

"What's wrong with him?" Zoe asks.

"He was soaking up some sun on the highway and was run over by a truck. The truck driver felt awful and brought the snake in to us," Gretchen explains. "He fractured several vertebrae. It has taken a couple of months, but Ralph should be ready for release soon."

"He's sort of beautiful, don't you think?" Zoe says. She brings her face close to the glass.

"I never thought about a snake being pretty before."

I'm impressed. I always figured Zoe for a snake hater. I guess you never can tell how people are going to respond to animals.

"What's wrong with this turtle?" I ask, moving to a smaller cage.

"Francis here will never be released." Gretchen lifts out a three-legged turtle almost the size of a lunch box. "He's a gopher tortoise."

That's right—a tortoise, not a turtle. Tortoises live on land, turtles live in the water. Duh.

"Gopher tortoises dig long burrows with their strong legs," Gretchen continues. "More than three hundred other species use gopher tortoise burrows for shelter, so they are an umbrella species. If they disappear, the other species will be hurt, too. Gopher tortoises were just designated a Species of Special Concern. That's what the government calls animals that aren't endangered yet but are dying out fast enough for us to be worried."

"What happened to his leg?" I ask.

Gretchen strokes the tortoise's shell. "A dog bit it off," she says. "We were able to save his life, but we can't release him. He can't dig burrows anymore."

"That's so sad," Maggie says.

"He's making the best of it," Gretchen says as she crouches down and puts Francis back in his cage. "He gets all the dandelions, strawberries, and sweet potatoes he can eat, and in the winter we make sure he's warm and snug."

A parrot in the corner caws loudly.

"Is there any kind of animal you can't take in?" Dr. Mac asks.

Gretchen stands up. "Cougars and bobcats. There's a rehab center farther south that specializes in them. We have the room but not the money. There's one whole wing of the building that we're not using yet. I'd love to set up exhibits and show kids more about habitat loss and the endangered and threatened species of Florida. Someday." She sighs. "When we solve the money problem."

Her words are hopeful, but she's not smiling anymore. I get the feeling that the center needs a lot more than nickels and dimes.

Dr. Mac and Gretchen lead the way back to the exhibit area. "I remember your plans when you were in vet school," says Dr. Mac. "You were going to specialize in marine mammals and move down here to the beach. You had visions of taking care of dolphins and spending lots of time waterskiing."

Gretchen chuckles as she holds the door open for us. "I haven't had a day at the beach in what, two years? If I don't get a call about an injury, or something with a bacterial infection, then I arrive in the morning to find a cranky alligator has been left on our doorstep. Or—and I swear this happened—I go out on a dinner date and end up chasing a seagull with a broken wing."

"Did you save it?" asks Zoe.

"The date?"

"No," Zoe giggles. "The seagull."

"Yes, as a matter of fact, I did," Gretchen says. "That's the part of this job I really love—the rescue, the hands-on work, the helping. I wouldn't change it for anything."

"Hang on," I say. "I'm confused. How can it be hard to get money for the center? It's so important to save and protect these animals."

"Some people get it," Gretchen says. "Floridians raise thousands of dollars every year from the sale of special SAVE THE MANATEES license plates, and we get donations from schools, scout groups, and families. But when you are trying to save a species on the edge of disaster, you are talking about big sums of money. Sometimes it feels like a race that we're losing."

"We can help," I say. "Tell us what you need done, and we'll do it."

Gretchen smiles. "I'd like to bottle that attitude. What I really need is about a hundred thousand dollars. I have a meeting with the bank tomorrow about a loan. I don't mind dealing with ornery alligators, but bankers scare the daylights out of me."

"It's not that bad, is it?" Dr. Mac asks.

Gretchen's smile vanishes. "Yes, it is, J.J. If I don't get this loan, we may have to close—even with a good turnout at the fund-raiser."

Close the center?

"I didn't realize it was so serious," Dr. Mac says. "Let me help. Why don't we go over your plans for the bank meeting?"

"That would be great," Gretchen says with relief. "Can you girls stay busy for half an hour?"

"I'm going to help wash out the boats," Maggie says.

"I'd like to keep an eye on Violet," I say.

"This is going to sound weird, you guys, but I'd love to take another look at that snake," Zoe says.

They all scatter, and Violet and I are left alone. I fiddle with my camera. I've got to get a shot of her swimming in the tank. But if I take a picture facing the glass, the flash will reflect back and ruin the picture. I slide to the side. Maybe if I take it from an angle...

Violet floats by. How could anyone hurt a beautiful creature like this? Manatees don't bother anybody. They just swim and eat and play. *Click!*

I read the sign posted next to the tank:

MANATEES ARE CLOSE TO EXTINCTION. AS MUCH AS TEN PERCENT OF THE POPULATION DIES EACH YEAR. LEADING CAUSES INCLUDE BOAT STRIKES, GETTING CAUGHT IN DAMS, HYPOTHERMIA, AND BACTERIAL INFECTION.

Ten percent!

My face flushes. It's not the heat—it's my temper. What would it take to get people to start paying attention? What would make them care? I wish I were older, old enough to move down here. I could start out volunteering, then Gretchen would give me a job. I'd find a way to tell people about the manatees—I know I would.

I lie down on the floor and angle my camera up so it looks like Violet is swimming above me, with shafts of light streaking down from above her. She has stopped swimming and is resting, floating straight up and down. Her flippers are suspended by her sides. Her chewed tail hangs gracefully. The stark white bandage covering those awful gashes looks like a big warning sign—TAKE CARE OF THIS CREATURE.

Click!

There has to be something I can do.

Chapter Six

• • • • • • • • • • • •

When Gretchen and Dr. Mac finish talking about the bank meeting, we drive to our hotel in Bay City. While Dr. Mac checks us in at the hotel's front desk, Maggie, Zoe, and I wander around the lobby.

I'm stunned.

"This place looks like a movie set!" I exclaim.

The lobby stretches twenty floors up to a glass ceiling and is longer than a football field. It reminds me of an expensive mall. It has two restaurants, fountains, a piano player, a bunch of little shops, and a special computer station where people can check their e-mail. In the middle of it all, a huge column of glass-and-chrome elevators rises up to the guest rooms above. Everywhere I turn there are glass windows, or mirrors, or other shiny surfaces that reflect my sweaty face and gaping mouth. I've stumbled into the Land of Oz.

"Do you believe this place?" I gush to Zoe and Maggie. "Your grandmother is nuts. It's got to cost a thousand bucks a night!"

"Relax," Maggie says as she falls into a poufy chair near a marble fountain. "It doesn't cost that much."

Zoe perches on the edge of the fountain. "I hope Gran lets us order room service," she says.

Something splashes behind her. "Look!" I say. "Fish!"

Big, fat goldfish swim lazily under a lily pad in the water fountain.

"Brenna, listen to me," Zoe advises. "You don't want to look like a hick. Act sophisticated. Look bored. Pretend that we jet all over the world. Compared to the Ritz in Paris, this place is a dump."

She rolls her eyes and pouts a little.

"Yeah, right, like you've ever been to the Ritz," says Maggie.

"I have," Zoe answers. "Mom and I flew to France for a fashion show last year. Now, this is how you have to act." She puts her hand up to her hair. "Ve must get zem to do zomesing about zees sunlight," she says in a fake French accent. "It's going to fade my hair color."

A bright green lizard crawls out from the plants surrounding the fountain and scoots over Zoe's lap. She shrieks. Maggie and I crack up.

"Way to go, Zoe," Maggie notes.

"Totally zophisticated," I add.

• • • • • • •

We have two connecting rooms with balconies that face the ocean. Maggie leaps onto the bed and turns on the television.

"Cool!" she shouts. "We have a million channels! We can watch three different baseball games."

Zoe is flipping through the room service menu. "We could have dinner either up here in the room or downstairs on the deck—the veranda, as they call it," she says. "I like the way that sounds: 'dinner on the veranda.'"

I slide open the glass door and step out onto

the balcony. From fifteen stories up, I can see the thin crescent of white beach, and beyond that the waters of the Gulf of Mexico stretching to the horizon. So much water! There are people bobbing and swimming close to the beach. Farther out, speedboats chase each other, and a few sailboats are pushed by the lazy breeze.

Are there any manatees out there? I'll have to ask Gretchen. I hope they stay away from the boats. I wish Violet had. It gives me the shivers to remember the way her back looked.

The door of the balcony next to me opens, and Dr. Mac steps out. She puts her hands on the railing and takes a deep breath of salty air.

"Beautiful, isn't it?" she asks.

"Sure is," I say. "I've never seen anything like it."

We stand quietly, listening to the mix of seagull calls and the faint noise of the children playing on the beach.

"Do you think Violet will be OK?" I ask.

"Gretchen is a gifted veterinarian, and the people on her staff are very smart. Violet is getting great care."

"I wish I could do more to help her," I say, twirling the manatee bracelet around my wrist.

"I understand," Dr. Mac says. "I wish more people felt the same way. So"—she slaps the railing to change the subject—"what do you think of Florida?"

I chuckle. "Honestly? I love it. The hotel is awesome, and the water, the palm trees, the birds. And our room! It's bigger than my house. You shouldn't be spending all this money, Dr. Mac. We could have stayed in a motel or at a campground."

Dr. Mac stretches her arms over her head. "I worked hard for my money, Brenna, and I don't spend it on fast cars or jewelry. But when I travel, I like to be comfortable. And I like being able to show you kids a little of the world."

She twists so that her back cracks, then reaches over to touch her toes. Dr. Mac is in good shape. She can lay her hands flat on the floor in front of her. "I still have kinks from those airplane seats. I'm going for a run on the beach," she says. "You girls stay out of trouble until I get back."

Maggie opens the door behind me and sticks out her head. "Can I call the clinic?"

"A fire?!" Maggie shouts into the phone.

"Ouch. Not so loud," Zoe tells her cousin. The three of us are crowded around one telephone.

David sputters on the other end of the line. "It wasn't my fault, honest, I swear," he says. "It was small, a small fire, a mini fire. Really just a couple of flames. And you'll be happy to know that the fire extinguisher works properly."

Someone takes the phone away from David.

"Hello? Dr. Mac? It's me, Sunita."

"Gran's not here," Maggie tells her. "Just Zoe, Brenna, and me. What happened?"

Sunita sighs heavily. I can just see her rolling her eyes in exasperation.

"I was sterilizing instruments in the autoclave, and it started to smoke," she explains. "Dr. Gabe took care of the whole thing. We were never in any danger, though David got a little excited with the fire extinguisher."

"Never a dull moment," Maggie chuckles with relief. "How's Sherlock?"

"And Sneakers?" calls Zoe.

"They're right here. I'll put them on." We can hear Sunita whispering something to the dogs, then their tags jingling, then *Rrowf! Awoooo!*

"Hi, baby!" Maggie coos.

"Sneakers! Sneaky-boy!" calls Zoe.

Oh, brother.

"It's me again," says Sunita. "I think they miss you guys. Even Socrates." Socrates is the MacKenzies' fat tabby cat. "He spends all his time sleeping on Dr. Mac's chair at the kitchen table. So tell me what the manatees are like!"

"You wouldn't believe what we did," I say, grabbing the phone. "We rescued this poor manatee that was hit by a boat! It was awful and wonderful all at the same time."

I describe the afternoon's adventures, with Maggie and Zoe filling in the details. "And I took lots of pictures," I assure Sunita.

"I can't wait to see them," she says. "Uh-oh, I've got to go. Dr. Gabe is calling me. Have fun."

Zoe presses down the little clicker to hang up the phone. "Do you want to call your parents?" she asks.

"Nope," I say. "Everyone's at work."

"Time to chill, then," Maggie says as she picks up the remote control and changes the channel. "Baseball!"

She leaps on the bed and leans against a pile

of pillows. "Stingers vs. Hurricanes. Top of the seventh, Stingers up four to three. Come here! You'll get to see Ronnie Masters, the home run hitter I was talking about."

"Gag," Zoe says. She picks up the little case with all her bathroom stuff in it. "I'm going to paint my nails."

I hop on the bed with Maggie. "Give me a pillow," I say. "I'll watch with you."

Dr. Mac opens the door that connects her room to ours. Her T-shirt is completely soaked with sweat, and her face is bright red.

"That was fast. Are you OK, Gran?" Maggie asks.

"Too hot," Dr. Mac puffs. She opens the tiny refrigerator and takes out a cold bottle of springwater. "Remind me to run early in the morning when it's cool out." She twists off the cap and drinks down half the bottle without stopping. "Ah, that's better." She holds the bottle to her forehead. "Who's winning?" she asks us.

"Stingers. Masters is up in a minute. Can we get room service?"

"I want shrimp!" Zoe calls from the bathroom.

"Why don't we just get a pizza or something?" I suggest.

Dr. Mac gulps down the rest of the bottle. "Gretchen and I planned a fun surprise for dinner," she says. "Much better than room service or pizza. But you'll have to put on something nice. Did you all bring a dress or a skirt to wear?"

"Impossible," Maggie says. "Something that requires a skirt cannot be fun."

Chapter Seven

● ● ● ● ● ● ● ● ● ● ●

The surprise is a sunset dinner cruise in the Gulf of Mexico.

"Don't you all look wonderful!" Gretchen calls from the top of the landing ramp. She's wearing a bright blue sundress, a lightweight yellow sweater, and sandals. Her hair is in a long braided ponytail, the way I usually wear mine, and her earrings are shaped like manatees. Very nice.

Maggie tugs at her skirt—a skort, really, a combination of a skirt and shorts. Getting her into it was nearly impossible. "I look stupid," she mutters.

"It's fine," Zoe says. "Quit pulling at it." Zoe has the perfect outfit, of course—a short black skirt, pink flowered top, and matching pink sweater.

My clothes don't match at all. My skirt is a disgusting shade of purple, and I'm wearing a shortsleeved white shirt with square black buttons up the front that keep clicking against my camera. It's a hand-me-down from my cousin in Vermont. Ugh.

I reach up to stick a stray bobby pin back in my hair. I made Zoe put it up in a bun like Gretchen's. It feels like there are little spikes in my head. I should have just worn my braid.

"This way, ladies," the hostess says.

The boat is really a floating restaurant. Every table has an awesome view of the water. Instead of windows, there are just railings. I'll be able to get lots of great pictures tonight.

As we walk to our table, I sneak a look at the other passengers. They are all really dressed up, the men in lightweight suits, the women in dresses, their hair perfectly styled. It's a big change from the rescue center.

"How's Violet doing?" I ask Gretchen as we take our seats.

Gretchen slowly unfolds her napkin and lays it in her lap. "She's still very stressed," she says. "That's not surprising, given what she went through. We hope her appetite will perk up by tomorrow."

"Is she in a lot of pain?" Dr. Mac asks.

"We gave her another shot of analgesic, a pain killer, before I left. After her second tube feeding, she started to look stronger. Manatees are pretty tough creatures. Do you know what land animals they're related to?" Gretchen asks. She stops to take a drink of water.

Maggie picks up the bread basket and passes it to Dr. Mac. "Their nickname is the sea cow, right? I bet they're related to cows."

Dr. Mac takes a roll and passes the basket to me. "Good guess, Maggie, but it's not right. Brenna?"

"I read this, but I didn't believe it," I say. "Manatees are related to elephants, aardvarks, and hydraxes, whatever they are." I take a slice of whole-grain bread and hand the basket to Gretchen.

"Quite a family, isn't it?" she laughs. "A hydrax looks like a guinea pig. It's a very distant cousin. Some people say that if you imagine a trunk and big ears on a manatee's head, you can see the resemblance to elephants."

"Is it true that people used to think that manatees were mermaids?" I ask.

Gretchen laughs again. She takes a piece of bread and butters it. "Back in 1493, Christopher Columbus recorded the first written description we have of manatees. He was bummed. The manatees were not the beautiful mermaids his sailors had promised him."

She pauses for a bite of bread. "Here's something you probably don't know. Legend tells us that the queen of the mermaids was named Ran. Her job was to watch out for girls and young women and keep them safe. And now it's our turn to watch out for the mermaids. I think that's neat. Now, what are we going to eat? I'm starved."

• • • • • • •

By the time the waiter brings our salads, the boat has left the dock and is puttering down the canal to the Gulf of Mexico.

Uh-oh. There are three forks by my plate, all different sizes. At my house we use only one fork per meal. Which one am I supposed to use? What if I use the wrong one?

I sneak a look at Gretchen. She takes the outside fork.

Phew! I sigh and copy what she's doing. Maggie, Zoe, and Dr. Mac are used to fancy hotels and restaurants, but I feel like a fish out of water. I'm going to stick to Gretchen and do whatever she does. That'll keep me out of trouble.

"Look at those houses!" Maggie exclaims, pointing with her fork to the mansions that line the canal. "They're huge!"

The pink, yellow, and light blue houses are all three stories tall. They have enormous decks built on every floor, swimming pools, and long docks with speedboats tied up at the ends.

"That's Mansion Row. This area has become really popular in the last few years," Gretchen explains. "The developers can't build houses fast enough. We're in a constant battle trying to preserve the natural habitat here."

Once we're past Mansion Row, we float by small islands crowded with birds. We give the waiter our orders and listen as Gretchen tells us about her days in vet school. As she starts to spill the beans about what Dr. Mac was like as a teacher, the noise of the boat's engines changes.

"Why are we slowing down?" I ask.

"This is a manatee area," Gretchen says. "See that sign?"

A sign sticking up from the water reads SLOW SPEED——CAUTION——MANATEE AREA.

I look over the railing. "I hope we'll see some."

"They might not be down there. It could be too cold. Manatees need to be in water that's warmer than seventy degrees Fahrenheit."

"Why?" Zoe asks. "They're so fat. I thought they had lots of blubber, like whales. Whales can swim in cold water."

Gretchen takes a sip of water. "That's a really good point. Whales can tolerate icy-cold ocean water because their blubber insulates them, keeping them warm like a winter coat. But manatees are tropical marine mammals. They have only a thin layer of blubber, and it doesn't insulate them well. To survive, they need to stay in warm water. Cold water can actually kill them. When it gets cooler, they gather together in warm river channels, natural springs, even the water outflow from power plants."

"Power plants?" I ask. "How bizarre."

"An unintended benefit of technology," Gretchen says. "The water that comes out of the power plants is just the right temperature for manatees. Of course, many are being closed now, and that cuts down on places where manatees can spend the winter."

The boat's engines whine louder, and we pick up speed as we pass a sign that reads LEAVING MANATEE AREA.

"Shucks," Maggie says. "I guess we're not going to see any."

"Keep your eyes open," Gretchen says as we pass under a bridge and by a fringe of beach. "We are officially in the Gulf of Mexico now. You girls will most likely see some dolphins."

"And here's dinner," Dr. Mac announces as the waiter sets a plate of steak in front of her. Maggie and Zoe both ordered shrimp. Gretchen ordered grilled tuna. I thought about it, but I'm used to tuna in a sandwich. I kept it simple: spaghetti and meatballs.

As I reach for my salad fork, the waiter takes it away. I look around. Everyone else is using the second of the three forks by their plates. When did they all learn these fork rules?

We eat quickly, enjoying the coastal breeze, the music playing over the loudspeakers, and the sight of the red sun setting in the western sky. It doesn't take long to finish our meal. I guess we were all hungrier than we realized. As the waiter brings out dessert—tangy Key lime pie—the crew turns the boat around and we reenter the canal, passing the manatee sign again, and slow down to a safe speed.

The captain, a tall, slim man wearing a white suit, strolls through the restaurant to make an announcement.

"If you care to look off the port side," he says, pointing to the left of the boat, "you'll see one of the wonders of Florida, a manatee calf."

We all drop our forks and head for the railing. I pause long enough to grab my camera.

"Do you see it?" I ask.

"Not yet," Gretchen says. "Look for the mother. She'll be easier to spot. They're sure to be together. Manatee calves depend on their mothers."

"Good thing we slowed down," Zoe says.

"There it is!" I shout. "By that buoy!"

I zoom in on the small lump with my camera lens and take a few shots. *Click! Click!* The baby manatee is only a few feet long. It's thrashing in the water, but it's not going anywhere.

"Something's wrapped around it. It can't swim," I say.

"Can I see the camera, Brenna?" Dr. Mac asks. I hand it to her.

"That calf is too young to be alone," Gretchen says anxiously.

"Maybe the mom is hunting for food or something," Zoe says.

"Manatees never leave their calves," Gretchen says. "Unless the mother is hurt, too. Or worse— dead."

"That calf is tangled in some kind of fishing rope," Dr. Mac says.

"Let me see," Gretchen says, reaching for my camera. She peers through the viewfinder. "Oh, no!"

"What's wrong?" I ask.

"We have to get him out of there," Gretchen says, kicking off her shoes and taking off her sweater. "He's close to drowning. Did you see the buoy floating near him? He's tangled in the rope that it's attached to. The rope probably leads down to a crab pot. And the tide is coming in."

I know what that means. The calf's snout is just barely out of the water now. When the tide comes in, the level of the water will rise and he'll be trapped under the water, unable to breathe!

The boat is drifting past the calf. Gretchen hands me the camera. "We've got to get him out of there," she says.

"I'll get the captain," I declare.

I run the length of the boat to where the captain is talking to an elderly couple.

"Please, sir," I interrupt. "You have to turn the boat around and go back. That baby manatee is in trouble. He needs our help."

The captain shakes his head. "Young lady, I'm sure the manatee is fine. This boat has to stay on schedule. Now if you'll please excuse me."

I grab his arm. "You don't understand. It's going to die! We have to go back!"

Splash!

"A woman just jumped in the water!" someone shouts.

I run back to the side. Gretchen is in the canal, swimming strongly toward the desperate calf. She's wearing a life jacket and towing a life ring.

My face flushes hot, my heart races. It's only

six feet down, a no-brainer. That manatee needs help. Now's my chance to make a difference.

I hand my camera to Maggie, climb on top of the railing, and dive into the canal.

Chapter Eight

. . . .

Brenna, stop right there!" Dr. Mac shouts from the boat as I come up for air.

I cough out canal water. *Yech!* It tastes oily and nasty. I'd better not think about what's in it. At least it's warm. I tread water for a minute, figuring out where I need to go.

"Brenna!" Maggie and Zoe scream.

I ignore them. The baby manatee and Gretchen need my help. I kick hard—*oops!* My sandals float off and sink to the bottom.

Don't think about it. Get to the manatee.

I pull with my arms and kick with my bare

feet, breaststroking so I can keep my face out of the water and my eyes on the calf.

"Brenna!" Dr. Mac shouts. "Get back here!"

A little voice in the back of my mind whispers, *Be a good girl.*

Sorry, Mom.

I swim faster.

Up ahead of me, I see that Gretchen has reached the calf. He's about the size of Maggie's basset hound. She lifts the baby manatee's head a few inches out of the water. His nostrils flare as he takes a big breath. The rope is wrapped tightly around his flippers and tail. He is really stuck. When Gretchen lets him go, he sinks back into the water, thrashing weakly. How are we going to get him untangled?

Gretchen has a worried look on her face.

I take three more strong strokes and pull up behind them.

Gretchen turns around, shocked. "Brenna! What are you doing here?" she demands. "Have you lost your mind? Swim back to the boat right now!"

That's not the greeting I was expecting.

"I came to help."

"Help?" she gasps. "Now I've got two of you to worry about."

The little voice in the back of my mind hollers, *You idiot! What did you think she was going to do—pat you on the back? Duh!*

By now, the boat has stopped in the middle of the canal. Dr. Mac and the girls are still shouting to me from the railing, crowded by all the other passengers. We've turned into a sideshow.

Gretchen looks at the manatee, back to the boat, then at me. *She's going to send me back.*

"I've got her!" she shouts back to Dr. Mac. "Here." She wiggles out of her life preserver and tosses it to me. "Put this on and buckle it. You might as well stay and help since you're here."

Another wave washes over the calf's head.

"What about him?" I ask as I slip into the life jacket and quickly buckle it. "No mother?"

She shakes her head no. "The calf is dehydrated. He's been alone for a few days."

"The water's rising," I say. "He doesn't have much time."

"Just as we thought, he's tangled up in the crab pot line," Gretchen explains. "All right, don't move. I'm going to see if I can move the crab pot."

She takes a deep breath and dives under. A wave from the boat's wake rolls in and crashes over the calf's snout. His nostrils open, and he snorts—a manatee cough.

The calf thrashes in the tangled rope. His eyes are moist and soft, crying out for help.

"You poor thing," I say quietly. "You must be so scared, out here all alone, not knowing where your mom is. Don't worry, we'll take care of you."

I reach out to the manatee, then stop. He pulls his head back and closes his eyes like he's afraid of me or something.

"I'm not going to hurt you," I say. "I came to rescue you."

He snorts.

Gretchen surfaces and takes a deep breath. "The pot is wedged under a rock," she says. "I can't budge it."

The manatee thrashes as water closes over his face. Gretchen holds his head up so he can breathe.

I swim a few strokes to the buoy. "We could unwrap him from this end," I say.

"Let's give it a shot." Gretchen cradles the calf in her arms, murmuring gently. "Try to be fast, but don't rush. If you tangle the rope more, we'll lose him for sure."

I kick my way to the buoy, a faded green plastic tube that bobs in the water. The rope attached to the buoy is snared in branches and tightly wound around the calf's flippers and tail. I have to untangle the rope from the branches, then carefully unwind it from around the calf while Gretchen holds him. It takes a few tense minutes, but finally, the calf splashes free.

"Excellent!" Gretchen says.

"Can we take him on the boat with us?" I ask.

"No. Carlos is on his way with the rescue boat. I told Dr. Mac to call him before I jumped in."

"Can I go with you?" I ask.

"No. Not a good idea, Brenna," she frowns. *Ouch.*

"I'm really, really sorry," I say. "I didn't want to make it harder for you."

Her frown softens a bit. "I know you didn't. Now, swim back to the boat. I'll stay with the calf." She glances over to where Dr. Mac is standing at the boat railing, her arms crossed over her chest. "And when you get on board, you'd better 'Yes, ma'am' and 'No, ma'am' J.J. all the way back to the hotel. She looks pretty steamed."

That's putting it mildly.

As the captain and a member of his crew haul me up the ladder at the side of the boat, Dr. Mac stands in the background, her face like a thundercloud. Someone puts a smelly blanket over my shoulders. My bun is destroyed, my hair hanging down in wet ropes, bobby pins sticking out everywhere. My clothes are soaked. My sandals are at the bottom of the canal. And I'm shivering.

Wait—my bracelet! *Phew.* Still there.

The slow, sputtering *Gordito* comes around the bend with one of Carlos's assistants at the wheel. At least the calf will be safe. I'm not so sure about me.

I follow Dr. Mac back to the table, leaving damp footprints on the carpet. Maggie and Zoe are busy staring at their dessert plates. I sit down without a word and use my napkin to wipe off my face.

"Are you OK?" Zoe asks as she sits next to me. "That was so brave."

"I didn't know you were such a good swimmer," Maggie says.

"Maggie, Zoe, find something to do," Dr. Mac

says. "Look for dolphins, flying fish, anything. Brenna and I need to talk. Alone."

Her right eyebrow is way up, a warning signal. I'm sunk.

My friends shrug their shoulders slightly. There's nothing they can do to help. They slip away, heading toward the bow.

I know I'm going to get it. I bet she puts me on the first plane home to Pennsylvania. No, it will be a bus or a train. Why did I do such a dumb thing?

The *Gordito* putters away ahead of us, with Gretchen and the calf loaded safely aboard.

"Do you think he'll be OK?" I ask. "He was really close to drowning."

Dr. Mac lines up her dessert fork next to her plate and turns the handle of her coffee cup so it's pointed north. She folds her napkin and lines it up next to the coffee cup. I should probably talk about something else.

"I'm sorry, Dr. Mac," I apologize. "I know I shouldn't have jumped in, but he was in trouble. I had to do something."

"Enough." She raises her hand. "I'm going to be blunt, Brenna. That was an incredibly stupid thing to do. Stupid and dangerous."

"But Gretchen... "

"But Gretchen, nothing. You should have let her handle the situation. She's the professional."

"I thought she needed help."

"She was fine. She is trained for these kinds of rescues. Did you notice that she put on a life jacket before she went in the water? Unlike you."

"There wasn't time."

"You put yourself in terrible danger. I know you care passionately about manatees, about any wild thing for that matter, but you won't help anything if you react on impulse. What would I say to your parents if something happened to you? You have to think, Brenna. Think!"

I glare at the growing puddle of water on my plate. My pie has turned to green, lumpy mush. I messed everything up.

"Are you going to send me home?" I whisper.

Dr. Mac sighs loudly. "No. It wouldn't make much sense. We're only here for a few days. But you"—she points her finger at me—"stay on dry land."

Ah-choo! I sneeze. "Promise."

Chapter Nine

· · · · · · · · · · · ·

We have breakfast the next morning on the hotel veranda overlooking the beach. Even though it's early, the veranda is crowded with families. The beach is busy, too. There are plenty of sunbathers and kids playing in the water. Farther out, sailboats glide gracefully in the sunshine. Speedboats dart around like hornets, their engines whining loudly.

Maggie concentrates on the choices in the buffet line. She ends up taking a stack of pancakes, two kinds of sausage, and the biggest glass of orange juice I've ever seen. Zoe takes a croissant, mango jelly, sliced kiwi, and apricot juice.

I'm not hungry. I hardly slept a wink last night. Even after showering, my hair still smelled like the canal. Maggie and Zoe tried to get my mind off how much trouble I was in, but I wasn't in the mood for popcorn and a video. I spent a long time on the balcony alone, listening to the surf washing over the sand, thinking about the gentle manatees swimming under the water, how much I wanted to help, and how stupid I was. It was not a good night.

I yawn, take a piece of wheat toast, and follow the others.

"Isn't this gorgeous?" Zoe says as she claims a table for us by the railing. It's shaded by a giant flowered umbrella that rocks back and forth in the ocean breeze. The air smells faintly of salt, clean and fresh.

"Yeah, it's nice," I say. I sit down across from Zoe and put my camera on the table.

"It's better than nice," Maggie says. "It's paradise with food." She puts a forkful of pancakes into her mouth. "Umm!"

"Aren't you hungry, Brenna?" Zoe asks.

I shake my head no. "Not really. When is she coming down?" Dr. Mac was on the phone when we left the hotel room.

"Soon, I guess," Zoe says. "Why?"

A waiter wearing a white jacket steps up to fill our water glasses.

"I'll tell you in a minute." I don't want to tell Zoe what's bugging me with a stranger around.

Maggie points over my shoulder. "Wow, look! That speedboat is really close to the shore."

I swivel around. The obnoxious roar of the engine gets louder as the red speedboat cuts a sharp turn that sends waves crashing to the shore. The kids in the water squeal with delight, but a couple of parents look annoyed.

"That's a monster," the waiter says. "Sounds like two hundred horsepower."

"That's the kind of crazy driving that kills manatees," I say hotly.

"Yes, it is," the waiter agrees. "But what can you do?" He shrugs.

The boat skips over its wake as the driver guns the engine. He's going way too fast.

Zoe frowns. "Are there any manatees out where that boat is?" she asks.

"Oh, sure," the waiter says. "I've seen them plenty of times. That guy definitely shouldn't be going so fast." He finishes topping off the water glasses. "Enjoy your breakfast, ladies."

"You're not enjoying anything, Brenna," Maggie says as the waiter moves on to the next table. "Come on, tell me. What's wrong?"

I sigh. "I still feel rotten about last night," I say. "Dr. Mac was furious. Gretchen, too."

"I think Gran was scared," Maggie says, spearing a sausage link. "I mean, you're her responsibility and all, and then you go leaping off the boat."

I pick up my toast and start to crumble it. "I know, I know, it was a totally stupid thing to do. All I could see was that poor drowning calf. And I thought Gretchen needed help." I drop the toast crumbs on my plate. "Dr. Mac must hate me."

Zoe delicately wipes kiwi juice off her fingers. "I wouldn't worry if I were you. Gran can get really intense when she's angry, but she still likes you. And it wasn't like you jumped off the boat for fun. You thought you were helping save an animal in distress. Gran's whole life is about saving animals."

"Here she comes," Maggie hisses.

Dr. Mac crosses the veranda balancing a cup of coffee, a notebook, and a plate mounded with fresh fruit. She's wearing khaki shorts and a purple polo shirt that matches the frames of her glasses. She doesn't look angry, but something's on her mind. She looks like she does when she's trying to figure out how to save a really sick patient.

I clear my throat. "Good morning, Dr. Mac," I say, trying to sound cheerful.

"Morning," she says absently. She takes the seat next to me, sips her coffee, and flips through the notebook, like she's looking for something.

"Is everything OK at the clinic?" Zoe asks.

"What? Oh, yes, I'm sure everything is fine," Dr. Mac answers without looking up.

"Earth to Gran," Maggie says, waving her hand in Dr. Mac's face. "Isn't that who you were talking to when we left? David didn't blow the place up or anything, did he?"

Dr. Mac takes off her glasses and lets them dangle from the beaded chain around her neck. "Sorry, girls, my mind is somewhere else. Frankly, the biggest problem they're having at the clinic is convincing Sneakers not to piddle in the kitchen."

"That's my biggest problem, too," Zoe says with a scowl. Her efforts to house-train her puppy, Sneakers, haven't been very successful.

"We'll deal with that when we get home," Dr.

Mac says. She takes a bite of the pineapple on her plate. "This is delicious. Toast? Is that all you're having, Brenna?"

I look at the pile of crumbs on my plate. "Not hungry, really."

"She feels bad about messing up last night," Maggie says.

"Maggie!" Zoe says.

I try to smile. "She's right." I turn to face Dr. Mac. "I'm so sorry about what I did. I hope you and Gretchen don't hate me. I'd like to go back to the center," I add quietly. "I want to see how the calf is doing—and Violet."

Dr. Mac stares at her pineapple like she didn't hear what I just said. What is going on? Is something wrong at the center? Is it Violet? Did the calf make it?

"Dr. Mac?"

She folds her glasses and puts them on the notebook. "Sure, Brenna. Apology accepted. Gretchen asked if we could spend the day helping them get the center ready for the fund-raiser. And she has the bank meeting today."

Dr. Mac is interrupted by the loud roar of a boat engine.

"Wow!" exclaims Maggie. "Did you see that?

I don't think I've ever seen a boat move so fast!"

I grab my camera and adjust the zoom lens so that I can see the boat speeding across the water. The people on board are all laughing.

The muscles in my arms and legs tense up. They aren't thinking about manatees. They probably don't even know what a manatee is! My face gets hot. I feel like racing down the beach, screaming at the top of my lungs for them to stop.

But that won't help.

I press my finger on the shutter release button.

Click! Click! Click! I got 'em!

• • • • • • •

As Dr. Mac drives us to the rescue center, I work on what I'll say to Gretchen. First, I'll apologize. Then I'll take a solemn oath never, ever to act without thinking again, and I'll swear to ask permission before I do or touch anything. Last, the begging. I'll beg forgiveness, beg her to let me help at the center until we have to leave, and beg permission to visit Violet and the little guy we rescued yesterday.

That ought to do it.

Dr. Mac turns into the Gold Coast lot. We park right by the front door (still no visitors) and walk in. A few volunteers are washing down the floor, and one is dusting the plaques on the wall. I head straight for the glass wall of the manatee exhibit.

Violet and the calf that was rescued last night are swimming in the exhibit tank. The calf looks like he's feeling much better. He swims fast— well, fast for a manatee—and twists around in a barrel roll.

"Look at him!" Zoe exclaims. "He's so cute!"

Violet drifts much slower, high in the water. She waves her right flipper once, but not the left one. Maybe it hurts too much because of the broken ribs on that side. The gashes the boat propeller made are still covered. Violet reaches one end of the tank, then slowly turns. There is lettuce floating in the water for her to eat, but she's not paying any attention to it. That can't be a good sign.

I stand next to the glass wall that separates us. "Come on, girl," I whisper. "Come on over here and say hi."

She doesn't notice me.

"We're going upstairs, Bren," Maggie says.

I could watch Violet all day, but it's time to face the music. I have to talk to Gretchen. I follow them up the stairs and into the tank room.

Carlos is kneeling by the manatees' tank, concentrating on his patients. One of the assistants is testing the water, and the other is taking notes at the desk.

"How are they doing?" I ask, crouching next to Carlos.

He points at the calf. "The little one spent the whole night eating. He's a strong one. Violet, well, she's having a harder time. I think she's leaking air into her chest cavity again. She seems to have a hard time diving. And I wish she would eat something on her own."

"Where's Gretchen?" Dr. Mac asks.

Carlos stands up and walks over to the sink, where he turns on the water to wash his hands. Something's up. He's stalling.

"The meeting at the bank didn't go as planned," he says finally.

"The loan?" Dr. Mac asks.

Carlos nods. "It doesn't look good."

Violet surfaces in the tank, snorting loudly. She drifts across the surface, looking like a lonely gray island.

Carlos dries his hands and tosses the paper towel through a tiny basketball hoop over the trash can. "Let's not worry about it now. I need one person to hose down the dock, someone to clean fingerprints off the exhibit wall, and someone to help me feed the calf."

"I'll feed the calf!" Maggie, Zoe, and I all say at the same time.

Carlos grins. "I thought that was going to be popular. We have to feed him every two hours, so you'll each get a turn. Let's do it alphabetically, Brenna first."

After the others leave, Carlos shows me how to pour the "baby formula" into a giant bottle.

"What's in this stuff?" I ask.

"It's a mixture of soy milk powder, water, and dextrose, which is a kind of sugar," Carlos says.

There's a splash and loud squeaking in the pool. The assistants are trying to get ahold of the calf to carry him out of the water. He thinks it's time to play.

Carlos takes a seat on a low stool near the edge of the pool, and his assistants gently place the calf in his lap. This would be a great photo, but I don't have time. It's time to feed the baby.

"How do I do this?" I say.

"He does most of the work," Carlos says. "Go ahead. Just put the bottle near his mouth."

I lower the nipple of the bottle to the calf's bristly mouth. *Shup!* He grabs onto it and starts sucking, hard.

Holding the bottle in one hand, I reach out with the other to touch the calf's back. It feels a little rough, like a football.

"They like to scratch," Carlos says. "We see them rubbing their backs up against rocks and ropes. That may be how this little one got tangled up in the crab pot line."

"How long will you have to bottle-feed him?" I ask.

"He can eat plants right now. They can do that from the time they're a few weeks old. But they still need the nutrition they get from their mother's milk. I'd like to find a female manatee who would adopt and nurse him. Manatees are great foster mothers. We'll call around to the other manatee facilities and see if they have any candidates."

"Can't Violet do it?"

Carlos looks at the injured female in the tank. "I had hoped that she would, but she hasn't responded to him yet. He keeps trying to get her attention, but she ignores him. Maybe when she's better. Look, he's falling asleep. My baby daughter does that when she's finished with her bottle, too."

The calf has let the bottle slip out of his mouth, and his eyes are closed. Manatees don't have eyelids like humans. The muscles around their eyes close up like a camera lens.

"You did a good job, Brenna," Carlos says.

"I think we should hire her."

I look up. It's Gretchen, standing in the doorway. She's wearing high heels, a skirt, and a blouse—the kind of outfit you wear when you have a big meeting with a banker. Maybe that explains why she looks so sad.

"How did it go?" I ask.

Gretchen shrugs and holds up her empty hands. "Not good. They're going to call later with their decision. It seems like everything is under control here, though."

"Brenna's a natural," Carlos says.

I fight back a smile.

"She needs to learn not to jump off of boats, but aside from that, she has all the makings of a marine biologist," Gretchen says.

I have to apologize—get the painful part over

with quickly. "I'm really, really sorry about last night," I say. "I should never have jumped off the boat or tried to help you without asking first. I just got carried away."

"Apology accepted," she says as she walks toward me, her shoes click-clacking on the cement. "The manatees are counting on people like you and me. They need us to be passionate, but they also need us to be smart."

I nod my head. She's totally right.

The calf jolts awake and squirms in Carlos's lap.

"Have you come up with a name for him yet?" Gretchen asks.

"I thought Brenna could name him. She's the one who spotted him first," Carlos says.

The calf opens his eyes and looks up at me. Hmm…what would be a good name? I scratch his belly while I try to come up with something. "What was the name of that great pie we had last night, the one I didn't get to finish because of my, ah, little adventure?" I ask.

"Key lime pie," Gretchen says.

"That's it, Key Lime. Is that a good name?"

Carlos grins. "A perfect name for a native Floridian. Now Key Lime here needs to go swimming. Which of the tanks do you want him in?"

"Has Violet interacted with him at all?" Gretchen asks.

Carlos shakes his head sadly. "He has tried to nuzzle up to her, but she doesn't like it."

"Has she eaten anything?"

"Not a nibble."

Violet swims by us in the tank.

"Her head looks better," I point out. "The peanut shape is gone."

Gretchen studies the injured manatee. "The tube feedings have started to rehydrate her and have given her some much-needed calories. But look at her position in the water."

Carlos nods. "She's leaking air into her chest again."

"I think the infection is getting the better of her." Gretchen takes off her earrings and watch and sets them on the counter. "Call everybody in. We're going to put her under to X-ray, tap the chest again, and clean out the propeller wounds. It's time for some manatee surgery."

Chapter Ten

· · · · · · · · · · ·

I've seen surgery at Dr. Mac's Place, but it's a
little different here. For one thing, the patient
weighs nine hundred pounds, so it's a bit harder
to move her around. It takes nearly an hour just
to get Violet into the treatment chute, put her in
the sling, drain the water from the chute, use the
crane to transport her into the treatment room
(with a very big operating table), and get her
ready for the anesthesia.

Maggie, Zoe, and I are allowed to watch as
long as we say on our stools in the corner. I
pretend my butt is stuck to the chair with gum.
I'm not going anywhere. Dr. Mac is scrubbed

and gloved, but mostly she'll just watch. She's the best pet vet around, but she doesn't have the experience with manatees that Gretchen and Carlos do.

Gretchen gives Violet a sedative in her peduncle, using a giant syringe with a long needle. With Violet relaxed, Gretchen, Carlos, and one of their assistants hook up Violet to a ventilator, a machine that will take over breathing for her while she's knocked out. Once that's all set up, they inject the strong anesthesia, and Violet is out like a light.

"Let's get to work," Gretchen says.

After scrubbing the left half of Violet's back, Gretchen makes a small incision through the skin and blubber. She takes a short piece of plastic tubing, about the size of a drinking straw, inserts it into the incision, and stitches it in place. It sticks out from Violet's skin just a little bit.

"This is a chest tube," she explains to us. "The tear in Violet's lung keeps leaking air into her chest cavity. When that cavity is full of air, the lung can't properly expand. We tapped it yesterday, but it filled again. This tube will make sure her lung can inflate properly."

"You mean she's going in the water with that

tube sticking out of her?" Maggie asks, her eyes wide. "Won't water get into the tube?"

"Maybe. The pressure from inside her body should hold much of the water out. It's the best we can do for now. We can't keep her on land until she heals. That'll take months. Manatees really shouldn't be out of the water for more than twenty-four hours. This is a better choice than allowing the lung to die. That would kill her for sure."

Gretchen takes a large syringe, sticks it into the chest tube, and pulls up on it. The tube slowly fills with some nasty-looking pus. She hands the full syringe to Carlos. He hands her an empty one.

"No wonder she was feeling rotten," Carlos says. "She has an infection in the chest cavity, too."

"I'm glad we caught it," Gretchen says as she suctions out more pus. "That's it. All gone. We'll increase her antibiotics to help kill this infection. The chest tube will allow for some drainage, too." She checks to make sure the chest tube is secure, then covers it with a small bandage fastened with superglue.

Carlos starts to peel off the huge bandage covering Violet's infected propeller cuts. "Since she's under anesthesia, we can really clean these cuts without causing her pain," he explains. He and Gretchen both pick up scalpels and start to cut away the dead tissue.

Zoe winces. "Are you sure that doesn't hurt?" she asks.

"She can't feel a thing right now," Gretchen assures her. She drops the scalpel on the instrument cart and picks up a brown bottle of disinfectant, which she pours into the open wound. "The contaminated wounds and lung problems are bad enough to kill her. We need to help her fight off this infection."

She rinses off the bubbly disinfectant, then pours on some more. "I'll do this a couple of times until I'm sure we've cleaned out all the contaminant," Gretchen explains. "This will help her form new tissue—scar tissue—that will close up the wounds."

Once Gretchen is satisfied that the propeller wounds are clean, she injects the drug that will reverse the anesthesia and wake Violet up.

"This is going to take a while," Gretchen says.

"I need to wean her off the ventilator, get her breathing on her own. Then we'll tube-feed her again and get her back in the tank."

"How long until we'll know if she's better?" I ask.

"We'll be able to tell right away if the chest tube is working. But it could take months or even years for a full recovery and until she's ready to be released. She's been through a lot."

One of the research assistants knocks and opens the door. "Phone call, boss," she says to Gretchen.

"Take a message," Gretchen says. "I'll call them back."

"It's the bank," the assistant says. "They said to tell you they're calling about the loan."

"We can finish up here," Carlos says. "Go."

Gretchen pulls off her surgical gloves with a snap. "Wish me luck."

"Should we release Key Lime into the tank with Violet?" Carlos asks as Gretchen heads for the door.

She pauses. "Absolutely," she says. "There's nothing like having a kid around to keep your spirits up."

While the staff gets Violet back in the water, Zoe, Maggie, and I are put in charge of going through the case histories of the wildlife treated at the center. Gretchen and Carlos have to write up a big report that lists all the animals they've treated in the past year, what they were able to release, and what died. It's the kind of paperwork the government requires.

Some of it is fascinating. They've saved alligators found in swimming pools, pelicans with fishing hooks in their beaks, deer that have been hit by cars, and an egret with a broken wing.

Some of it is sad. A sandhill crane run over by a drunk driver. A manatee that had some jerk's initials carved into its back with a knife. Three baby river otters deliberately killed.

But we focus on the good stories, not the bad, and the work goes quickly. When Carlos brings in boxes of hot pizza for dinner, none of us can believe that the entire afternoon has flown by. He sends me to find Dr. Mac and Gretchen.

Dr. Mac is sitting on the edge of the dock with her feet in the canal. Gretchen is sitting next to her.

"Pizza's here," I say. "You'd better come if you want any."

"Have a seat, Brenna," Dr. Mac says, patting the deck next to her.

Uh-oh. It's that serious, grown-up tone of voice again.

"What's wrong?" I ask as I sit down.

Gretchen tucks a loose strand of hair into her bun. "The bank won't loan us any more money, and we can't afford to pay back what we already owe," she says. "The rescue center has to close."

Close the center? They can't!

"No!" I shout.

Dr. Mac knows what I'm feeling. "I realize that sounds drastic, Brenna. We've been trying to come up with an alternative all day."

"You can't close this place!" I exclaim. "What about Violet? And Key Lime? And the snakes and alligators? They'll die without you. Doesn't the bank know that? Go to a different bank. And what about the fund-raiser? Dr. Mac is giving you money. Everyone is giving money."

"I wish it were that simple," Gretchen says. She pries a sliver of wood up from the dock. "This isn't the first bank I've gone to—it's the ninth. And Dr. Mac has been very generous, but we need really big bucks. Checks with lots of zeros on the end. It costs thirty thousand dollars to care for one manatee for a year. And our equipment is very expensive. Some of it isn't paid for yet, and the rest has to be maintained. The money just isn't there."

The insects have quieted down. The only sounds are the faint radio playing for the snakes and tortoises inside and the gentle slap of the river against the hulls of the rescue boats.

Gretchen rubs her hands over the wooden dock to feel for more slivers. "I'm sorry. I didn't mean for this to happen."

I try again. "But Violet... "

"We'll work it out. I'll talk to the other critical-care centers and see who can take our manatees. We'll find homes for the other critters, too. Then I have to help my staff find jobs... "

She stops, her voice choked with emotion. Dr. Mac reaches out and squeezes her hand. Gretchen clears her throat.

"The bankers are coming here tomorrow morning. They want to inspect the property."

Dr. Mac lifts her feet out of the river and shakes the water off them. "We'll stay out of your hair," she says. "The girls are ready for some beach time, and I have tickets to the baseball game tomorrow."

"Did you cancel the fund-raiser?" I ask.

Gretchen collects the slivers in the palm of her hand. "The fund-raiser is still on," she says. "We still need every dime to cover our debts. I'll make the announcement there. I hope you can come." She looks over at me. "It will be your last chance to say good-bye to Violet and Key Lime."

Dr. Mac stands up and motions to me with her hand. We should leave Gretchen alone.

"I'll save you a slice of pizza," I say as I get to my feet.

"Um-hmm," Gretchen answers.

We leave her at the water's edge.

Chapter Eleven

. . . .

After breakfast the next morning, we head for the beach. Maggie and Zoe both glop on handfuls of thick white sunscreen.

"You'd better put some on, too," Maggie says as she tosses me the bottle of lotion. "You don't want to take a sunburn home as a souvenir."

Zoe stretches out on her towel. "Ah, the sun! Don't you love it?"

I rub sunscreen on my arms and face. This is an awesome beach. The sand is clean and dotted with shells left by the tide. There aren't any noisy motorboats out yet, and the breeze keeps things cool. Still, I wish I were at the rescue center instead.

"I'm going swimming," Maggie announces. She leaps up, sprints to the water, and dives in. She shouts for me to join her.

"No, thanks!" I call back.

Zoe sits up and crosses her legs. "Brenna Lake, I know you're bummed, but this is a vacation. You are supposed to have fun. F-U-N spells fun."

I pick up a shell and draw a manatee in the sand. I've got the manatee blues. "I keep thinking about the center. I can't believe it has to close."

Zoe fills her hands with sand and opens her fingers to let it dribble out. "I know, but they're going to take care of the animals. Carlos told us about the other places that they can go."

I wipe away the sand manatee with my hand. "It's not right. I can't help being sad about it."

"That's 'cause you're a good person," Zoe says.

Maggie flops down between us. "The water is great! You guys don't know what you're missing."

"Brenna's bummed about the center closing," Zoe says. "I'm trying to cheer her up."

"It stinks, I know," Maggie says as she squeezes

the water out of her pigtails. "But Gran said they tried everything. Sometimes things don't work out. Come swimming with me. That will make you feel better."

* * * * * * *

After lunch, we pick up my photos from the FotoHut and head for the ballpark with Dr. Mac. The Bay City Stingers are playing the Hurricanes again.

Yippee.

We wade through the huge crowd to take our seats in the stands. This is only the Stingers' second season. The ballpark is pretty spiffy. It has two giant twenty-foot-high screens in the outfield and comfortable seats. We're ready for the game: popcorn, cotton candy, and nachos with cheese.

But all I can think about is the center. What will happen to Key Lime if he doesn't find a mother? Is Violet strong enough to be moved to another center? Who will answer the next manatee rescue call? I can't shake all the questions out of my head.

Maggie, however, is in sports heaven. "Stingers are going to win," she says confidently. "I can just feel it."

"Nope, you're wrong," Zoe says. "The Hurricanes will win."

"You don't know anything about baseball," Maggie protests.

"They won the last time, didn't they?" Zoe says, peeling off a strand of pink cotton candy.

"Who are you rooting for, Dr. Mac?" I ask.

"I'm neutral territory," she says. "How about you, Brenna?"

I shrug and eat a handful of popcorn. It doesn't matter who wins, as long as they do it quickly. If the center had half the money spent on this ballpark, they could save hundreds more manatees.

The Hurricanes bat first and get one run. Good, that was fast. Stingers at bat. The first player strikes out. The second one gets to first base, then moves to second when the third Stinger hits a single. It's Ronnie Masters's turn.

The crowd starts to chant. "Ron-nie! Ron-nie! Ron-nie!"

"Here he comes!" Maggie shouts. She turns to me, totally pumped. "He hit fifty-two home runs last year and batted .312!"

Zoe rolls her eyes.

"Come on, Ronnie!" Maggie screams. "Bang one out of the park!"

Great. He's going to hit a home run, and we'll be stuck in this inning forever.

Ronnie steps up to the plate and takes a practice swing. His face fills the giant screens in the outfield. The pitcher throws the ball. Ronnie swings.

"S-s-strike!" calls the umpire.

The giant screens zoom in on Ronnie's face again.

Wait a minute.

"I've seen him before," I say.

"Yeah, right. On TV in the hotel room," Maggie scoffs.

"No, really. I mean in person. Can I see the program?"

Dr. Mac passes it down to me. I flip quickly through the pages. Here he is:

RONNIE MASTERS: OUTFIELD, LEADS THE LEAGUE IN HOME RUNS, ACQUIRED IN THE OFF-SEASON, PLAYED FOR PHILADELPHIA FOR FOUR YEARS.

There is a half page of statistics that Maggie probably knows, then a quote from the home run king himself:

I LOVE FLORIDA. THE WEATHER IS GORGEOUS, THE PEOPLE ARE FRIENDLY, AND THE FISHING IS SPECTACULAR.

Under the quote is a picture of Ronnie and his family on his boat. A red speedboat.

"It's him!" I shriek, pointing to the picture. "The guy on the boat. Remember, yesterday? That obnoxious speedboat at breakfast? *He* was driving."

"No way," Zoe says.

"Yes way," I insist. "Wait, I can prove it!"

I rip open my backpack and rummage around in it. I pull out the envelope from FotoHut and flip through my photos: the airport, Sunita and David, the palm trees we saw on the first day, Violet, little Key Lime struggling in the canal, and...

"Bingo! Here he is driving the boat that was buzzing the beach yesterday! Remember? We talked to that waiter about it."

Maggie reaches for the photo. "I don't believe it."

"See for yourself," I say as I hand it to her.

On the field, the Hurricanes' pitcher winds up and throws again. Ronnie swings.

"Strike two!"

Maggie peers closely at the boat photos. Zoe needs just one glance. "Yep, that's him," she says. "No doubt about it."

Dr. Mac slips on her bifocals and leans over to look for herself. "They're right, Maggie. Mr. Masters may be a great home run hitter, but he's a lousy boat driver."

"I can't believe it," Maggie says as she hands the picture back to me. She looks a little shaken up and sad. "I thought he was a good guy. When he played for the Phillies he was always visiting sick kids in the hospital, being a great role model. I can't believe he would do something so stupid."

She looks down at home plate. Ronnie waits for the next pitch. "I hope he strikes out," she says.

The pitcher fires a fastball across the plate.

Crack!

"Home run!" bellows the announcer over the

loudspeaker. The crowd around us leaps to their feet, shouting and whistling. Ronnie jogs around the bases and stomps on home plate with both feet.

"What a loser," Maggie grumbles.

• • • • • • •

By the end of the game, Ronnie Masters isn't just a loser. Maggie thinks he's the biggest jerk who ever lived in the history of the universe. Me? I've got a bone to pick with him.

"I suppose you girls don't want to stand in line for Ronnie's autograph now," Dr. Mac says as we leave our seats after the final out.

Maggie tosses her empty popcorn box in the trash. "Gross. I wouldn't touch anything signed by him."

"I do," I say firmly. "Dr. Mac, will you wait for me?"

"Are you sure?" she asks, puzzled.

"Positive," I assure her.

"Why?" Zoe says. "You saw what he did."

"You'll see," I promise.

The line in the autograph area is fairly short, probably because the Hurricanes ended up beating the Stingers, 9 to 4. Ronnie Masters and his teammates sit behind a long table, signing whatever is put in front of them. A guy in a Stingers jacket is in charge of keeping the line moving. His I.D. badge says PUBLIC RELATIONS.

"Next!" he calls, waving to me.

OK, Lake, I tell myself. *You can do this. Keep cool—don't lose your temper. Think before you act.*

"Hi," I say as I step up to the home run king.

"Well, how ya doing?" Ronnie asks, flashing a million-dollar smile. "Do you have something for me to sign?"

"I have a picture of you," I say. "I took it myself, yesterday. This is your boat, isn't it?" I slide my photo across the table.

Ronnie looks at the picture. "Yes, it is. That's a pretty good picture there. You going to be a photographer when you grow up?"

Here we go. Be smart.

"Mr. Masters, you were driving your boat too fast," I say politely. "There could have been manatees out there. I want to show you something else."

I flip through the stack of photos until I get to Violet in the river. "See these horrible gashes? They were caused by the propeller of a speedboat. I don't know who did it, and I'm not accusing you.

But this is what unsafe driving does. Manatees are an endangered species. There are only a couple thousand of them left."

"That's enough," interrupts the guy directing the line. "Everybody needs a turn. Let's go."

Ronnie holds up his hand. "Hang on, Stu. Give her a chance."

I pull a flyer for the rescue center's fund-raiser and a brochure about manatees out of my backpack.

"Could you read this stuff, please?" I ask. "My friend Maggie said you were a good guy. Maybe you just don't know about manatees yet. You're new around here. This center saves manatees and lots of other wildlife. But they need help."

"Mr. Masters can't make any promises to endorse or support anything," says Stu, the annoying guy in the jacket. "Thank you for your time. I'm sure he'll consider it. Next!"

I don't move. "People look up to you, Mr. Masters. You can make a difference."

Ronnie Masters quickly signs his name on a trading card and hands it to me with my photos. "I'll think about it," he says.

"Next!"

Chapter Twelve

• • • • • • • • • • • •

The rescue center is half filled with people by the time we arrive for the fund-raiser. Most of the guests are the volunteers and interns who work at the center, plus their family and friends. A Jimmy Buffet disk is playing on a CD player set up on the reception desk.

Next to the desk is a table with munchies and punch on it. Someone strung a few blue, green, and purple streamers across the lobby to try to dress it up a bit. It actually makes it more depressing, maybe because I know this is the last party that will be held here. I should have left my camera in the hotel room. I don't feel much like taking pictures.

Maggie and Zoe head for the food table. I ate too much at the ballpark. Dr. Mac crosses the room to talk to Gretchen, who is chatting with Carlos by the donation box. It doesn't look like much money has been added to it. I'm going to give all my change before I leave.

Gretchen smiles as Dr. Mac greets her, but she looks beat. Between trying to save the manatees and the rescue center, I don't think she's getting much sleep.

Key Lime and Violet look like they're dancing above the heads of the small crowd. Violet still has her propeller cuts covered by bandages, but it looks like she's moving her left flipper a little more. I hope that means she's not in as much pain. She gracefully floats across the tank like a queen, while Key Lime darts, twirls, and spins around her like the court jester, still trying to get her attention.

Gretchen catches my eye and points to the door that leads upstairs to the pool room. Does she want me to go up there? I point to my chest—me? She nods, opens the door, and heads up the stairs.

She's waiting for me at the top.

"Do you need me for something?" I ask when I get there.

"You didn't look like you were having a good time," she says as she sits on a stool by the sink.

"Well, it's kind of sad," I say.

"I agree. Want to help me feed Violet?"

"Sure! I'd love to. What do I have to do?"

"I'll show you." Gretchen stands up and opens the refrigerator. I cross the room and take the vegetables that she hands me—heads of romaine lettuce, bananas, and sweet potatoes.

"You can wash the lettuce while I cut up the potatoes," she says.

I turn on the water and rinse the lettuce. "It looks like she's swimming more comfortably. Is she eating better, too?"

Gretchen cuts the sweet potatoes into quarters. "Much better. The antibiotic kicked in, and her appetite came storming back. When we changed her bandage this morning, there were hardly any signs of infection."

"I'm ready," I say, holding up the lettuce.

"Go ahead and put it in the tank," Gretchen replies.

I toss a chunk of lettuce into the water.

Violet surfaces for a breath and investigates the lettuce with her sensitive snout. Then she uses her flippers to bring the lettuce into her mouth and devours it.

"I wish we could feed them by hand," I say.

Gretchen chops up some more potatoes. "I know. That's what everyone says. But that's being selfish, thinking about what we want, not what's best for them. Violet is wild. We owe it to her to let her stay that way."

I sit cross-legged at the side of the tank. "What's going to happen to them when you close?" I ask quietly.

"I spent most of the day on the telephone finding homes for everyone," Gretchen says. "Key Lime is going up to a zoo in Ohio. They've taken in young calves before and cared for them until they were big enough to be released back down here. We'll keep Violet here for a couple of weeks. Then we'll send her to a rehab center in Sarasota. The staff there takes great care of their animals."

She tosses pieces of sweet potato into the tank.

"What about the gopher tortoise, and the red

rat snake, and the others?" I ask. "They need good homes, too."

"I'm still working on it. There are small zoos and some schools I need to talk to." She peels a banana and tosses it in the water. "We also have to help our interns and researchers find a new place to work." She peels a second banana and offers it to me. "Want one?"

"Sure." I take the banana. Across the tank, Violet grabs her banana, too. It disappears in one gulp. I eat mine one bite at a time.

"I tried to talk to a boater today," I say. "I saw him driving too fast in a manatee zone."

"How did it go?" Gretchen asks as she peels a banana for herself.

"I think I blew it. I showed him pictures of Violet's injuries and tried to explain why it's important to pay attention to the signs posted in manatee waters, but I don't think he was listening. He thought I was just another dumb kid. It makes me so mad. Everyone says that kids are the future, but no one wants to listen to us."

Key Lime surfaces near us, his tiny nostrils twitching. He takes a deep breath and dives again.

"Don't let that discourage you," Gretchen says. "You're a smart, resourceful girl, the perfect manatee protector. You're going to grow up into one of those people who make a huge difference. You're already doing that, just by talking to people and educating them about the needs of manatees and other wildlife. It might not be as dramatic as diving off a boat to save a calf, but in the long run, it will be more significant." Gretchen winks at me, then nods toward the tank. "You can give her some more lettuce."

I toss two more heads of romaine into the water.

The crowd noise coming up from the stairwell is getting louder. If I look down into the tank, I can see the people moving around through the glass wall, a few faces peering into the water to look at the manatees.

Gretchen stands up. "I'd better tell them, break the news about closing the center. It sounds like they're getting restless down there."

"Do you really have to close it? There's nothing else to do?"

Gretchen tosses the last of the sweet potatoes into the water and sighs. "This has been coming

for months, Brenna. It didn't just happen over-
night. I should have been more realistic, planned
better. I kept hoping that something would turn
up—a grant or a hefty donation from someone's
will."

She washes her hands in the sink and dries
them on a towel. "But it's over. If we can't pro-
vide the animals with the best quality care here,
then they need to go someplace else." She hangs
the towel on a rack neatly so it will dry. "Are you
coming downstairs?"

Violet surfaces briefly for a breath. She's so
beautiful, propeller scars and all.

"No, I'll stay here, if that's OK."

"Sure," Gretchen says. "I understand." She
leaves without another word.

Violet slowly glides across the tank, her flippers waving back and forth. The little fingernails
on the ends of her flippers look like elephant
toenails. Dr. Mac says that fifty million years ago,
manatees lived on land. Manatees and elephants.
Now both are endangered.

A burst of laughter comes from the lobby.
Obviously Gretchen hasn't given them the news
yet.

"Brenna?" Dr. Mac calls as she jogs up the stairs. "There you are. You've got to come downstairs!"

"No, thanks," I answer. "I'd rather stay here as long as I can. I'm not in the mood for a party."

"You will be in a minute." She crosses the room, takes my hands, and pulls me up to my feet. "I promise, you'll want to see this."

The crowd downstairs has grown bigger. In fact, it's twice as big as it was when I left. There are three photographers with enormous cameras hung around their necks, chowing down on the last of the corn chips. The Jimmy Buffet music is playing louder, and everyone looks relaxed, almost happy.

"Where did all of these people come from?" I ask Dr. Mac.

She puts her finger to her lips, her eyes sparkling. Something is up.

Gretchen turns off the music and blows into a microphone. Her eyes are red. It looks like she's been crying.

"Excuse me," she says. "Can I have your attention, please? Everyone? I have a few things to say."

Dr. Mac leads me to the front of the crowd.

Maggie and Zoe squeeze past the crowd to join us.

"Do you guys know what's going on?" I ask.

Maggie opens her mouth, but Zoe covers it with her hand. "You promised," she warns her cousin. "You'll find out in a minute," Zoe tells me.

This is getting weirder and weirder.

Gretchen takes a deep breath as the crowd quiets. "Thank you," she says. "What a night. I came here with a speech all written in my head. I was going to tell you what an amazing place this is..."

Everyone claps.

Gretchen smiles. "But you already know that. You also know this center has one of the best staffs in the world, dedicated people who have devoted their lives to saving our wildlife. And I've had the pleasure this week of spending time with the next generation of wildlife lovers. The future is in good hands."

Maggie, Zoe, and I all turn bright red as everyone stares at us and applauds.

Gretchen waits for quiet again.

"I was going to come up here tonight to tell you that the Gold Coast Rescue Center was closing." She holds up her hands as some people gasp in surprise. "We weren't kidding when we said we needed your donations. In fact, I spent the day making plans to transfer our animals."

She stops, too choked up to speak. She clears her throat.

"But the rescue center was just rescued! I'd like to introduce my new best friend, Ronnie Masters, of the Bay City Stingers baseball team. Ronnie?"

No! It can't be! No way!

Ronnie Masters works his way up to the microphone. Following him is Stu, the public relations man, and a few of Ronnie's grinning teammates carrying small children. The photographers abandon the corn chip bowl and start snapping pictures.

Ronnie takes the mike. "Thanks, Gretchen. I'll make this short. I'm not much for speeches. I'd been looking for a good charity to support since I came down here a few months ago. Someone," he winks at me, "suggested this might be a good place."

Maggie elbows me in the ribs. *Is this really happening?*

"The Stingers have agreed to donate five thousand dollars to the center every time I hit a home run," Ronnie continues. "I'm throwing in five thousand of my own for each run I hit. So far this season, I've hit forty-five, so I guess we owe you four hundred and fifty thousand dollars."

WOW!

Tears stream down Gretchen's cheeks. Carlos is crying, too. The crowd explodes into shouts, whistles, and applause. I stare at Maggie and Zoe. "What did he say?" I stammer. "Four hundred and fifty thousand dollars? How can he give so much money?"

"His new contract pays him nine million dollars a year," Maggie says. "Trust me, he has it."

"It's not happening," I say.

Dr. Mac laughs. "Yes, it is," she assures me.

Ronnie motions for us to quiet down. "Stu, here, wants to say something," he says as he hands the microphone to the Stingers' public relations man.

"Ronnie kind of sprung this on us at the last minute," Stu says, "but when the big man speaks, we listen."

He pauses to clear his throat. Everyone is quiet. "Ahem. The Stingers want to support the Gold Coast Rescue Center as one of our official charities. We'll be making plans for Manatee Day at the ballpark and will work with you to develop an advertising campaign to alert our fans about safe boating, not polluting the water, and protecting Florida's wildlife."

The crowd cheers loudly, cutting off the last thing he says. Gretchen steps forward, taking the mike again.

"Brenna, will you come up here, please?"

Me?

"Go on, go on!" Maggie says, giving me a little shove. I walk up to Gretchen, who turns me around to face the crowd.

"This is the hero of the hour, folks," Gretchen says. "Brenna Lake. She's responsible for all of this."

The photographers all point their cameras at me. *Click! Click! Click! Click! Click!* The flashes are blinding.

Gretchen says a few more things, then hands the mike to Carlos. To be honest, I can't hear them. There's an ocean roaring in my ears, all the feelings of the past few days building up and crashing over me. I finger my manatee charm.

I did it!

I did something that really made a difference. Too bad there's not enough room to turn a cartwheel in here.

I look up at the manatees swimming on the other side of the glass wall. While Violet munches on her lettuce, Key Lime swims close to her. She leans forward, touching her muzzle to his. I freeze. She's talking to him!

Key Lime nuzzles his way along the side of her head and down her right side. Violet lifts her right flipper. Key Lime noses his way to her nipple and starts to nurse. She's feeding him!

I tug on Gretchen's arm and point. The crowd quiets, Carlos stops talking, and everyone turns to stare. The orphaned calf and his foster mother float together peacefully.

I bring my camera up to my face and quickly adjust the focus for the best picture of Florida.

Click!

Make Room for Manatees

BY J.J. MACKENZIE, D.V.M.

Wild World News—Florida manatees are the most endangered coastal marine mammals. Researchers think there are fewer than 3,000 of them left, and we're losing 10 percent of the manatee population every year.

In order to save them, we first have to understand them. Studying these large mammals is a challenge. Because they are endangered, manatees cannot be captured for the sole purpose of study. So a lot of what we know about manatees comes from observing the animals while they are recuperating from life-threatening injuries at rescue or rehab centers. Teams of researchers also study them in the wild, but they are careful to keep their distance and not disturb the manatees' environment.

UNDERSTANDING MANATEES

Now hear this. Knowing how manatees hear might be the key to saving them from boat strike injuries. Because manatees communicate in high-pitched noises, researchers suspect that they don't pick up the low-pitched noise made by a boat engine until the boat is very close. That may explain why some manatees can't get out of the way in time to avoid a collision.

Curious creatures. Manatees are very curious. When they see a strange object in the water, they naturally want to inspect it, play with it, and in the case of fishing line or rope, even floss their teeth with it! But their curiosity often gets them into trouble. They become entangled in fishing nets or lines, eat trash that may kill them, or become exposed to harmful pollution or waste.

A hazardous habit. Manatees like to scratch their skin by rubbing against rocks, floating branches, ropes, and the bottoms of boats. They might be doing this to leave their scent so other manatees know they've been there. Or they might be doing it because it feels good. Whatever the reason, this habit is dangerous because it brings manatees to the surface where boats may be.

Nature calls. Of course, manatees also die from natural causes. If the water gets too cold, they go into hypothermic shock and die. A few years ago, an algae bloom called *red tide* killed several hundred manatees by poisoning their nervous systems.

FOLLOW THAT MANATEE

Locating and keeping track of the number of manatees is very important. Researchers observe migration patterns, make notes about new calves, track rehabilitated manatees, and take regular population counts.

Tiny bubbles. Some researchers use equipment called a *hydrophone*—a type of underwater microphone—to track manatees under the water. With their diet of vegetation and their superlong intestines, manatees produce a large amount of gas. When it's released, it creates a lot of tiny bubbles in the water. Scientists use the hydrophone to listen for the bubbles. And where there are bubbles, there will likely be manatees!

Show your scars. Once manatees are located, scientists try to identify them. Researchers can tell manatees apart by the scars they have from boat accidents. This "scar catalogue" is constantly being updated with pictures taken by researchers and volunteers. The catalogue is an important tool for tracking manatees and learning more about them.

Phone home. Some manatees wear a tracking device fastened around their peduncles. Signals from the device are sent to satellites orbiting the earth. Scientists receive the satellite information and can track where the manatees are swimming. This teaches us about migratory paths, activity habits, and where manatees like to live.

Playtime. By tracking their migration patterns, researchers have learned that manatees are semi-social animals. Except for hanging out with their mothers when they are young, manatees spend most of the year alone. This changes in the wintertime, when manatees gather together in warm springs, sometimes in groups of 100 or more. During these gatherings the manatees "play" together. They nuzzle each other, play follow-the-leader, and bodysurf. In follow-the-leader, the pack mimics the lead manatee exactly. They twist, dive, roll, and come up for a breath one right after another, squeaking and chirping.

THE BIGGEST THREAT

Researchers and volunteers work hard to help manatees, but humans are still the manatees' biggest threat. The warm waters that shelter manatees also attract people who build houses close to the water and drive motorboats. Boat strikes cause many manatee injuries and death. Much work is being done to educate boaters and residents about the dangers they pose to manatees, but there's still a long way to go.

WHAT YOU CAN DO TO HELP

Even if you've never seen a manatee before, you can help protect these gentle giants by joining the Save the Manatee Club.

The club (SMC) sponsors the very popular Adopt-a-Manatee® program. When you adopt a manatee, you will receive a photo of your manatee, an adoption certificate, information about manatees, and the club newsletter. Your adoption fee will be used to help pay for research, rehabilitation, and education programs. For more information, contact:

Save the Manatee Club
500 North Maitland Avenue
Maitland, FL 32751
www.savethemanatee.org

Joyce Tenneson

In addition to the Vet Volunteers series, **LAURIE HALSE ANDERSON** is the author of the multiple award-winning, *New York Times* best-selling novel *Speak*, as well as *Catalyst* (an ALA Top Ten Best Book for Young Adults), *Prom*, and *Twisted* (both *New York Times* Best Sellers). She lives in northern New York with her husband and their dog.

Visit her Web site at **www.writerlady.com**.